Fourth Victim
by

Kathi Daley

I want to thank the very talented Jessica Fischer for the cover art.

I so appreciate Bruce Curran, who is always ready and willing to answer my cyber questions, Jayme Maness, who helps out with my book clubs and special events, and Peggy Hyndman, for helping sleuth out those pesky typos.

And, of course, thanks to the readers and bloggers in my life, who make doing what I do possible.

Thank you to Randy Ladenheim-Gil for the editing.

And finally I want to thank my sister Christy for always lending an ear and my husband Ken for allowing me time to write by taking care of everything else.

Books by Kathi Daley

Come for the murder, stay for the romance.

Zoe Donovan Cozy Mystery:
Halloween Hijinks
The Trouble With Turkeys
Christmas Crazy
Cupid's Curse
Big Bunny Bump-off
Beach Blanket Barbie
Maui Madness
Derby Divas
Haunted Hamlet
Turkeys, Tuxes, and Tabbies
Christmas Cozy
Alaskan Alliance
Matrimony Meltdown
Soul Surrender
Heavenly Honeymoon
Hopscotch Homicide
Ghostly Graveyard
Santa Sleuth
Shamrock Shenanigans
Kitten Kaboodle
Costume Catastrophe
Candy Cane Caper
Holiday Hangover
Easter Escapade
Camp Carter
Trick or Treason
Reindeer Roundup – *December 2017*

Zimmerman Academy The New Normal
Ashton Falls Cozy Cookbook

Tj Jensen Paradise Lake Mysteries by Henery Press:

Pumpkins in Paradise
Snowmen in Paradise
Bikinis in Paradise
Christmas in Paradise
Puppies in Paradise
Halloween in Paradise
Treasure in Paradise
Fireworks in Paradise – *October 2017*

Whales and Tails Cozy Mystery:

Romeow and Juliet
The Mad Catter
Grimm's Furry Tail
Much Ado About Felines
Legend of Tabby Hollow
Cat of Christmas Past
A Tale of Two Tabbies
The Great Catsby
Count Catula
The Cat of Christmas Present
A Winter's Tail
Taming of the Tabby
Frankencat
The Cat of Christmas Future – *November* 2017
The Cat of New Orleans – *February 2018*

Seacliff High Mystery:
The Secret
The Curse
The Relic
The Conspiracy
The Grudge
The Shadow
The Haunting

Sand and Sea Hawaiian Mystery:
Murder at Dolphin Bay
Murder at Sunrise Beach
Murder at the Witching Hour
Murder at Christmas
Murder at Turtle Cove
Murder at Water's Edge
Murder at Midnight

Rescue Alaska Paranormal Mystery:
Finding Justice – *November 2017*

A Tess and Tilly Mystery:
The Christmas Letter – *December 2017*

Road to Christmas Romance:
Road to Christmas Past

Writers' Retreat Southern Mystery:

First Case
Second Look
Third Strike
Fourth Victim
Fifth Night – *January 2018*

The Writers Retreat Residents

Jillian (Jill) Hanford

Jillian is a dark-haired, dark-eyed, never-married newspaper reporter who moved to Gull Island after her much-older brother, Garrett Hanford, had a stroke and was no longer able to run the resort he'd inherited. Jillian had suffered a personal setback and needed a change in lifestyle, so she decided to run the resort as a writers' retreat while she waited for an opportunity to work her way back into her old life. To help make ends meet, she takes on freelance work that allows her to maintain her ties to the newspaper industry. Jillian shares her life with her partner in mystery solving, an ornery parrot with an uncanny ability to communicate named Blackbeard.

Jackson (Jack) Jones

Jack is a dark-haired, blue-eyed, never-married, nationally acclaimed author of hard-core mysteries and thrillers, who is as famous for his good looks and boyish charm as he is for the stories he pens. Despite his success as a novelist, he'd always dreamed of writing for a newspaper, so he gave up his penthouse apartment and bought the failing *Gull Island News*. He lives in an oceanfront mansion he pays for with income from the novels he continues to write. He does not live at the retreat at this point, but his relationship with Jill brings him to the retreat on a daily basis. He is also an integral part of the Mystery Mastermind Group, a name he came up with to describe the writers who join together to solve mysteries.

George Baxter

George is a writer of traditional whodunit mysteries. He'd been a friend of Garrett Hanford's since they were boys and spent many winters at the resort penning his novels. When he heard that the oceanfront resort was going to be used as a writers' retreat, he was one of the first to get on board. George is a distinguished-looking man with gray hair, dark green eyes, and a certain sense of old-fashioned style that many admire.

Clara Kline

Clara is a self-proclaimed psychic who writes fantasy and paranormal mysteries. She wears her long gray hair in a practical braid and favors long, peasant-type skirts and blouses. Clara decided to move to the retreat after she had a vision that she would find her soul mate living within its walls. So far, the only soul mate she has stumbled on to is a cat named Agatha, but it does seem that romance is in the air, so she may yet find the man she has envisioned.

Alex Cole

Alex is a fun and flirty millennial who made his first million writing science fiction when he was just twenty-two. He's the lighthearted jokester of the group who uses his blond-haired, blue-eyed good looks to participate in serial dating. He has the means to live anywhere, but the thought of a writers' retreat seemed quaint and retro, so he decided to expand his base of experience and moved in.

Brit Baxter

Brit is George Baxter's niece. A petite blond pixie and MIT graduate, she decided to make the trip east with her uncle after quitting her job to pursue her dream of writing. Her real strength is in social networking and understanding the dynamic behind the information individuals choose to share on the Internet.

Victoria Vance

Victoria is a romance author who lives the life she writes about in her steamy novels. She travels the world and does what she wants to who she wants without ever making an emotional connection. Her raven-black hair accentuates her pale skin and bright green eyes. She's the woman every man fantasizes about but none can ever conquer. When she isn't traveling the world she's Jillian's best friend, which is why when Jillian needed her, she gave up her penthouse apartment overlooking Central Park to move into the dilapidated island retreat.

Nicole Carrington

Nicole is a tall and thin true crime author with long dark hair, a pale complexion, and huge brown eyes. She has lived a tragic life and tends to keep to herself, which can make her seem standoffish.

Garrett Hanford

Garrett isn't a writer, but he owns the resort and is becoming one of the gang. He had a stroke that ended his ability to run the resort as a family vacation spot but seems to be on the mend and has plans to move back to the resort. He has lived on Gull Island his entire life and has a lot to offer the Mystery Mastermind Group.

Townsfolk:

Deputy Rick Savage

Rick is not only the island's main source of law enforcement, he's a volunteer force unto himself. He cares about the island and its inhabitants and is willing to do what needs to be done to protect that which he loves. He's single man in his thirties who seldom has time to date despite his devilish good looks, which most believe could land him any woman he wants.

Mayor Betty Sue Bell

Betty Sue is a homegrown Southern lady who owns a beauty parlor called Betty Boop's Beauty Salon. She can be flirty and sassy, but when her town or its citizens are in trouble, she turns into a barracuda. She has a Southern flare that will leave you laughing, but when there's a battle to fight she's the one you most want in your corner.

Gertie Newsome

Gertie Newsome is the owner of Gertie's on the Wharf. Southern born and bred, she believes in the magic of the South and the passion of its people. She shares her home with a ghost named Mortie who has been a regular part of her life for over thirty years. She's friendly, gregarious, and outspoken, unafraid to take on anyone or anything she needs to to protect those she loves.

Meg Collins

Meg is a volunteer at the island museum and the organizer of the turtle rescue squad. Some feel the island and its wildlife are her life, but Meg has a soft spot for island residents like Jill and the writers who live with her.

Barbara Jean Freeman

Barbara is an outspoken woman with a tendency toward big hair and loud colors. She is a friendly sort with a propensity toward gossip who owns a bike shop in town.

Brooke Johnson

Brooke is a teacher and mother of two who works hard in her spare time as a volunteer coordinator for the community. She first met Jack and Jill when she was a suspect in the first case they tackled.

Sully

Sully is a popular islander who owns the local bar and offers lots of information about the goings-on in the community. When Blackbeard manages to escape for a day on the town, one of the first stops he always makes is to see his buddy Sully.

Quinten Davenport

Quinten is a retired Los Angeles County Medical Examiner who is currently dating Gertie. Although retired, Quinten is more than happy to help the Mystery Mastermind Group when they need a medical opinion, and his presence provides stability to them.

The Victim

Francine Kettleman

Frannie lived in a cabin at the Turtle Cove Resort from April 1963 to August 1964. She moved there after her husband, Tom, was drafted and sent overseas during the Vietnam Conflict. During her stay at the resort she received love letters from a man named Paul, who was also stationed in Vietnam. Fifty-three years later, the letters, which she tied in a ribbon, placed in a metal box, and hid in the wall of one of the cabins, were found by the contractor in charge of the remodel of the resort. In August 1964 Tom was injured and sent back to the States. On August 14, 1964, Frannie became the fourth victim of the Silk Stocking Strangler, who murdered thirteen women over a ten-month period. All the victims were strangled with a pair of women's silk stockings, their bodies found in cemeteries along the East Coast from Florida to Massachusetts. The Strangler was never caught and the murder cases were never closed by the FBI.

The Other Players from 1964

Tom Kettleman

Frannie's husband at the time of her death. He has since passed away, but those who remember him say he came back from Vietnam not quite right. It is rumored that if Frannie hadn't been killed, she may very likely have died at the hands of the man to whom she was married.

Paul Kettleman

Tom's brother and believed to be the man behind the letters. As far as anyone knows he is still alive, but no one knows his current whereabouts.

The Silk Stocking Strangler

The person believed to have murdered thirteen women over a ten-month period from 1964 to 1965, all with a pair of women's silk stockings, all found in cemeteries along the East Coast from Florida to Massachusetts. The Strangler was never caught and the murder cases were never closed by the FBI.

The Suspects and Witnesses

Ned Colton

Ned was the deputy in charge on Gull Island when Francine Kettleman went missing. Because Frannie was believed to be a victim of a multistate mass murderer, the FBI was the lead agency in the investigation. The FBI was certain Frannie was the fourth victim of a killer who would ultimately kill thirteen women, but Ned found some irregularities in her case that led him to question whether she died at the hands of the Strangler or a very clever copycat.

Sherry Pierce

Sherry was a friend of Frannie's who still lives on the island. She knows a secret about Frannie no one else does, a secret she has kept to this day.

Edna Turner

Edna is a retired librarian who knew Frannie when she lived at the resort and still lives on Gull Island.

Roland Carver

Roland was the mayor of Gull Island at the time Frannie was living at the resort and still lives on the island. While on the surface he seems to be willing to share what he knows, it seems obvious he is guarding a secret.

Clint Brown

Clint owned a local real estate agency at the time of Frannie's murder. He seems willing to cooperate but, like Roland, he seems to have a secret.

Wes Gardner

Wes is a lifetime Gull Island resident who once owned a used bookstore. He often sat and chatted with Frannie when she came in each week to check out the new inventory.

Chapter 1

Monday, December 11

"Fifty-three years ago, Francine Kettleman—Frannie K for short—lived at the Turtle Cove Resort while her husband, Tom, was away in Vietnam. Frannie, who was just nineteen when she arrived on Gull Island, lived there from April 1963 to August 1964. During her stay, Frannie received love letters from a man named Paul, who was also stationed in Vietnam. Years later, the letters, which Frannie had tied together with a ribbon, placed in a metal box, and hidden in the wall of the cabin where she was living, were found by the contractor in charge of the remodel of the resort. After a cursory investigation, we know that on August 14, 1964, Frannie was found dead in a cemetery fifty miles from here. It's believed by most that Frannie was the fourth victim of the Silk Stocking Strangler, a mass murderer who was never caught or identified. The Strangler was credited with killing thirteen women over a ten-month period from

1964 to 1965. All the victims were strangled with a pair of women's silk stockings, and all were found in cemeteries along the East Coast from Florida to Massachusetts."

I paused to look around the room at the people who had gathered to hear my proposal. I could see this case had everyone's attention. Love, intrigue, and tragedy all wrapped up in one package. We'd stumbled upon the letters Frannie had left behind before Thanksgiving, so we were familiar with the specifics, but in the interest of tradition, it was the task of the submitting author, who in this case is me, Jillian Hanford, to officially present the case to the other members of the Mystery Mastermind Group.

"Are you asking us to track down a serial killer?" Alex Cole, a fun and flirty millennial who made his first million writing science fiction when he was just twenty-two, asked.

I turned to answer him. "Not at all. If Frannie was indeed killed by the Strangler, finding her killer is beyond our ability to research."

"Is there any doubt Frannie was a victim of this madman?" Brit Baxter, a blond-haired pixie and aspiring writer of chick lit, asked.

"While I haven't yet come up with any hard evidence that would indicate Frannie wasn't the fourth victim of the Silk Stocking Strangler, I do have reason to question that assumption. I recently met with Ned Colton, who was the deputy in charge on Gull Island when Frannie was murdered. Given the fact that her body was found fifty miles away, and the FBI was already investigating the Silk Stocking Strangler, Ned wasn't asked to take an active part in this investigation. Ned shared with me that he took the liberty of looking in to things on his own. He admitted that, on the surface, it appeared Frannie *had* been murdered by the Strangler, but there were some anomalies he found interesting."

"Anomalies?" Victoria Vance, a romance author who lives the life she writes about in her steamy novels and my best friend, asked.

"The Silk Stocking Strangler had a signature of sorts. He always abducted his women at night, he used silk hosiery to strangle his victims, and he always chose women who were blond, blue-eyed, and between the ages of twenty and twenty-four. He always left the bodies of his victims in a graveyard and he always posed them lying on their back with their arms across their chest. He also always left a single red rose lying across the victim's neck."

"And does that match what happened to Frannie?" Victoria asked.

"It does. To the letter."

"So why does this Deputy Colton think she may not have been a victim of the Strangler?"

"Little things, really. For one thing, the Strangler was strong. The women he strangled died quickly, and it appeared he came up on them from behind because none of them had any defensive wounds. Frannie, however, appeared to have fought back. She had a bump on her head and defensive wounds on her hands and arms. While the autopsy didn't detail any discrepancies between Frannie and the other women, it was Ned's opinion she died much more slowly than the others, which could indicate the person who strangled her wasn't as strong or as skilled as the real Strangler."

"Did Deputy Colton consider the idea that Frannie was stronger than the other victims and therefore better able to fight back? That could have led the Strangler to be less effective in his attack." Jackson Jones—Jack for short—a dark-haired, blue-eyed, never-married nationally acclaimed author of hard-core mysteries and thrillers and my current love interest, asked.

"Yes, he did," I answered. "That was what the FBI believed. The difference in the killings could even be explained by something as simple as the Strangler being under the weather and therefore off his game. Ned told me that based on the data provided in the report it seemed as if Frannie may even have been knocked out and then strangled."

"So she fought back, either fell and hit her head, or her killer hit her in the head, causing her to pass out before being strangled," George Baxter, a writer of traditional whodunits, summarized. "That seems like a pretty big discrepancy to me."

"Ned and I agree. We both feel this case should have been given more attention than it was by the individuals investigating the Strangler."

"What else did the deputy have?" Jack asked.

"Ned also told me the roses the Strangler left were a long-stemmed, thornless variety. The rose left with Frannie's body was long stemmed and red like the others but not thornless."

"Maybe he couldn't find a thornless rose when he killed Frannie," Brit speculated.

"No," Clara Kline, a self-proclaimed psychic who writes fantasy and paranormal mysteries, countered. "We've since learned that serial killers are very methodical. They have a ritual that's very important to them that must be adhered to exactly if they're to obtain the emotional satisfaction or psychological relief normally brought to them from the kill. A serial killer wouldn't simply make a substitution. I think that's an important clue."

"I agree with Clara, but it seems the FBI should have come to the same conclusion," Jack stated. "Why didn't they suspect a copycat?"

"Because of the tattoo," I said. "The Strangler carved a pentagram on the back of the right shoulder of every woman. The FBI kept that piece of information out of the press, so no one other than law enforcement knew about it. Frannie had the mark on her shoulder, the same as every other woman. What I'm asking you to do is help me determine whether Frannie K was the fourth victim of the Silk Stocking Strangler or if she was killed by someone else who used the hype created by the serial killer to try to get away with murder. I know the anomalies are small, but according to Deputy Colton, the FBI determined Frannie was a victim of the Strangler and never considered any other suspects."

"Do *we* have other suspects?" George asked.

"Not really," I admitted. "At least not yet."

"Were you ever able to identify the man who wrote the letters?" George asked.

"I've been unable to definitively identify him, but Deputy Savage managed to obtain the original FBI report. While the Paul in the letters never gave his last name, the FBI determined Frannie's husband Tom had a brother named Paul. While we don't know this for certain, we're assuming the writer of the letters was Frannie's brother-in-law. We haven't been able to track down Paul Kettleman to verify it."

"And Tom?" George asked.

"We've been able to confirm that in August 1964 Tom was sent back to the States after suffering a head injury. Five days after he arrived in South Carolina, Frannie was dead. Tom died eleven months after Frannie was murdered due to complications from the head injury he received in Vietnam."

"So if the Strangler didn't kill Frannie, her husband must have done it," Brit surmised.

"Maybe. Based on the letters Paul sent, he was concerned for Frannie's safety when Tom came home, although it may be hard to prove he killed her. We certainly won't be able to get a confession from him. Still, we do have something to work with. Ned has expressed an interest in working with us should we decide to pursue the case. He has the file he created at the time of the murder, which he feels should be reexamined. Additionally, I've gathered the names of several people who still live on the island who knew Frannie when she lived here. I thought we'd speak to them. If we can get a better idea of exactly what was going on in Frannie's life at the time she was killed, other suspects may begin to emerge. Jack and I have already decided to take a stab at figuring this out. Is anyone else in?"

The room fell quiet. I decided to give everyone a minute to process what I'd shared with them. It was a lot to take in and a lot of years had passed. This wasn't going to be an easy case to tackle.

"Mystery solved, mystery solved," Blackbeard, my brother Garrett's parrot, broke the silence.

I laughed. "It looks like Blackbeard's in." I looked at the large bird. "I guess I should have asked you if you had anything to add." Blackbeard had been instrumental in solving mysteries in the past, although he most definitely hadn't been living at the resort when Frannie had. I doubted he was even alive, though parrots could live eighty or more years and I had no idea how old he was, so I supposed it was possible. Garrett had told me that he'd found Blackbeard, or more accurately, Blackbeard had found him. Garrett had been near the beach when Blackbeard flew up and landed on his shoulder. They'd been friends ever since.

"The solution to this mystery isn't going to be that easy," Brit joined in. "You all know I'm involved in the local production of *A Christmas Carol*, which runs from December 20 to December 22. We have an aggressive rehearsal schedule until then, so I'm not sure to what extent I can help, but I'm happy to if I can. My specialty is really social media and I don't think that will come into play in a fifty-year-old case, but if you need me to research anything, just holler."

"Thanks," I responded. "I appreciate that."

Alex spoke next. "As you know, I'm pretty busy trying to finish my book on Trey Alderman, but if you need something specific, just ask."

"I have some time," George said. "I'm digging into my books, but I can do some research on the Strangler. It does seem like an interesting case."

"Great; thanks." I smiled.

"You know I'm in," Vikki said, jumping onto the bandwagon. "I've been captivated by Frannie's story since you first showed me the letters. I think we can depend on help from Rick as well." Vikki was referring to Deputy Rick Savage, the acting deputy in charge on the island and Vikki's current love interest.

"We've discussed the matter a few times and I can tell he's intrigued."

"And I as well," Clara voiced. "You can't help but wonder what really happened to that poor woman. I've been meditating on the necklace you found with the letters and I think I'm close to establishing an emotional link with her spirit."

"Okay. Let's decide on a date so whoever's available can get back together. Jack and I have interviews set up for the next two days and then we're working at the tree lot on Wednesday afternoon. How about Thursday or Friday?"

"Friday evening works best for me because we don't have rehearsal then," Brit said.

"I can do Friday," Vikki seconded.

Everyone else agreed, so we set Friday evening at six for our next meeting. I volunteered to make dinner. George requested lasagna and Clara wanted garlic bread, so it seemed we had our menu.

"I think that went well," Jack said as Clara headed upstairs and everyone else left for their cabins.

"I feel really drawn to this case. It's just so tragic. Whether Frannie was murdered by a serial killer or someone she knew and possibly loved, she was still just twenty years old. Twenty is much, much too young to have your life stolen from you."

Jack put his arm around my shoulders and pulled me close. "We've got a solid starting place and, I feel, a very good chance of finding out what really happened to Frannie."

"You sound optimistic."

"You know me: Jack Optimistic Jackson."

I smiled. "I do rather love that about you. So, where should we start?"

Jack removed his arm from around me and took a sheet of paper from his pocket. "Here are the interviews for the next two days. I'm between novels, but I do have a paper to run, so I thought I'd work in the mornings and we could sleuth in the afternoons. We won't have a lot of time on Wednesday; we're supposed to be at the tree farm at four."

"What do we have tomorrow?"

"I know you spoke to Ned Colton on the phone, but I thought we should get a look at his file and maybe pick his brain a bit. I made an appointment to meet him at his home at one o'clock. I can pick you up at noon and we could grab a quick lunch first."

"That sounds good. Anyone else tomorrow?"

"Edna Turner. As you know, she was the town librarian at the time Frannie was murdered. When we spoke on the phone she told me that Frannie was an avid reader who came in to the library often. Edna expressed what seemed to be genuine grief over Frannie's death and indicated she was willing to help however she could. She seems to know a lot of people and I'm hoping she'll give us some additional leads. We're meeting with her at three o'clock. I thought we could go back to my place after that. I seem to remember you mentioning a willingness to help me decorate the place for the holiday."

"Sounds like fun. I think I may start decorating the resort tomorrow morning as well. As for tomorrow night, let's do pizza. I've been craving a good pizza for days."

"It's a date." Jack leaned over and gave me a quick kiss on the lips.

"And what does Wednesday look like?"

"I've made two appointments for the early afternoon. We're seeing Sherry Pierce, who was a friend of Frannie when she lived on the island, at noon, and Roland Carver, who was the mayor at the time of the murder, at two o'clock. After that we'll need to head to the tree lot for our shift."

"I can't wait to get started."

After Jack left I grabbed a sweater and went out onto the patio. It was a clear night and the stars in the sky looked like diamonds on a bed of black velvet. The nights had grown cooler as the days had grown shorter, but I still enjoyed spending a few minutes looking out over the vastness of the ocean before I went to bed.

I loved the fact that I could hear the sea from my bedroom in the attic. It was calming to let the natural rhythm of the waves lull me to sleep. When I'd first moved to Gull Island from New York, I'd missed the sound of traffic, but now that I'd been on the island for six months the hustle and bustle of the city didn't possess the same appeal it once had.

"I see you had the same idea I did," Vikki said as I walked slowly along the white sand beach.

"It's a lovely evening," I agreed. "I'll admit the warmer climate doesn't quite mesh with the idea of Christmas, however."

"We should decorate the resort. We can string white lights on the patio and around the eaves of the cabins. The main house will be a bit more challenging, but I'm sure we can get the guys to help."

"I've been thinking about decorating. I'd love to do a tree in the living room of the main house. There are some boxes of decorations in the spare room. I'll take a look tomorrow to see what we have. Will you be here for Christmas?"

"I'm planning to spend Christmas Eve and Christmas Day with Rick. We're invited to his brother's for Christmas dinner."

"We should have a big dinner here at the resort earlier in the week. Maybe the twenty-third?"

"Alex is going to the Bahamas on the twenty-third. How about the twenty-second? Brit's play is wrapping up that night, but it's an early performance, so she should be done by seven. We can have a late dinner afterward."

"I love the idea. I'll check with the others." I looked out toward the calm sea. "I think I'll head in. I'll see you in the morning."

"I'm heading out early to meet with my agent. I'll stop and stock up on twinkle lights while I'm in Charleston. Maybe we can start decorating tomorrow evening. I can't wait to turn this place into a Christmas fairyland."

I went back into the house, locked up, and headed up to my room. I grabbed some pajamas from my dresser and went into my attached bathroom. I changed and washed up, then went back into the bedroom. I was tired and it was late, but for some reason I was oddly antsy. Deciding to watch TV for a few minutes, I dug around in my nightstand for the remote. A piece of paper fell to the floor as I pulled out the remote from the drawer. Leaning over, I picked it up and was about to toss it back in the drawer when I noticed the message, penned with pink ink. It was a reminder I'd made to myself to follow up on a lead I'd been provided regarding a freelance article I planned to write detailing the secret behind a real-life local Santa. Restaurant owner Gertie Newsome had told me about the legend a week earlier and it had immediately piqued my interest.

It seemed that twelve years ago a fire on the north end of the island had destroyed four homes. Three of them were vacation homes, but the fourth was a primary residence, and the family who lived there had lost everything. The fire had occurred just a week before Christmas, making the pain of loss all that much more acute. The family didn't have insurance that paid for a temporary rental and it looked as if they might be homeless until an anonymous donor paid for a furnished rental nearby. When the family arrived at their temporary home, not only was the home fully stocked with food, clothing, and other items they'd need, but there was a large decorated tree in the living room with dozens of colorfully wrapped gifts placed beneath.

The person who'd saved Christmas for this family was never identified and it was assumed the benefactor's generosity was a onetime thing. The story was mainly forgotten until the next year, when the local animal shelter was about to be shut down due to the loss of their facility, until Secret Santa, as everyone began calling him, anonymously donated an alternate building that was still being used to this day.

Every year since, a person, family, business, or animal in need had been gifted with their own Christmas miracle. Jack had written a nice article for the local paper, but if I wanted to interest a national publication in the story, I'd need to dig deeper to identify the person behind the legend. My mind played with exactly how I would accomplish this as I drifted off to sleep with a smile on my face.

Chapter 2

Tuesday, December 12

Clara was sipping a cup of tea when I went downstairs the following morning. Her cat, Agatha, was curled up by the fire and looked about as content as a cat could be. "It looks like we're in for some rain," I said as I glanced out the window while I waited for my coffee to brew.

"I heard we're in for at least an inch," Clara confirmed. "It's a fast-moving system with a lot of wind, so I expect we'll be back to sunshine by tomorrow."

Given the fact that I had agreed to spend four hours in an outdoor tree lot on Wednesday, back to sunshine was exactly what I was hoping for.

"I was going to take Blackbeard to visit Garrett this morning, but animals aren't allowed inside the facility, so I guess I'll have to postpone."

"It'll be better when he's home for good," Clara commented.

"The last time I spoke to Garrett, he indicated his physical therapy was going well and he planned to spend a week or more with us over Christmas. If that goes well, he plans to speak to his doctor about making a permanent move back to the resort."

Clara gazed into the distance as if in a trance. "It's his home. It's where he should be." She blinked and then glanced back at me. I wondered where she went off to when she faded away like that.

I took a sip of my coffee. "Jack has been working hard to make sure the house is completely accessible to Garrett when he comes for the holiday. We want him to be as independent as possible." I took a look around the cozy building I now thought of as home. "Vikki and I talked about decorating the resort. She's in Charleston today and is going to stop to get lights for the patio and cabins. We may have to wait to put them up until the rain passes, but I think it will look lovely when we're done."

Clara's face lit up. "Oh, I agree. It'll feel magical."

"In the meantime, I thought I'd start with the interior of the main house. Do you want to help?"

"I'd love to." Clara smiled. "When I was a girl my mother had a little village she set up every year. The houses had lights that illuminated the interior so you could see the detail inside. I remember sitting for hours looking at that village. I'd make up stories about what the residents of those little houses were up to. Such wonderful memories."

"It does sound wonderful. Where are those houses now?"

Clara frowned. "I'm not sure. When my mother passed, my sister took them, but I'm not sure what happened to them after that."

"You have a sister? You've never mentioned her. Or any family, for that matter."

"I had a sister. She's gone now. They all are. I'm afraid it's just me."

"I'm so sorry." I squeezed Clara's hand. "You have us now."

"I do, and I'm very happy to be here and to help you bring some Christmas cheer to the place. Do you have decorations?"

"I moved boxes of stuff from the attic to the small bedroom at the end of the hall when I remodeled. I remember seeing some decorations. I thought I'd start there and then maybe head into town to get whatever else I need. I need to meet Jack at noon, though, so I don't have a lot of time, but this morning seems like as good a time as any to get started."

"It would be nice to bring some Christmas cheer to the place. Not that the house isn't perfectly lovely the way it is, but it's been a while since I've had a tree."

"Will you be here for Christmas?" I asked.

"I have nowhere else to be."

"George and Brit are going to Brit's parents' house for the holiday and Alex is taking his model of the moment to the Bahamas, but none of them leave until the twenty-third, so I thought we'd have a big dinner here on the twenty-second, after Brit's play."

"That sounds nice. I do so enjoy it when we all get together. If Garrett is coming home, I assume you won't be traveling over the holiday?"

I shook my head. "Jack is going to stay here for the long weekend, so it will be him, Garrett, and us for Christmas Eve and Christmas Day."

Agatha got up from her spot by the fire, crossed the room, and jumped into Clara's lap. "And Victoria?" Clara asked.

"She's spending Christmas Eve and Christmas Day with Rick and his family. Let's take a look at those boxes. I usually don't bother to decorate for Christmas, but this year I can't wait to get started."

When I moved into this house at the resort I'd decided I wanted to convert the large, airy attic into a private suite, so I'd moved everything stored there into one of the smaller bedrooms. I hadn't touched anything since, so when we entered the room I had to take a moment to try to remember where I'd seen the decorations.

"I think they might be on that back wall, but I'm not sure," I said as I made my way across the room, lifting the lids of boxes as I passed to take peeks inside. "Why don't you look in the boxes near the closet? One of us will come across the items we're looking for."

While some of the boxes contained old clothing and discarded household items, others contained mementos gathered and stored away by past residents of the large house. The property on which the resort had been built had been in Garrett's family for several generations, and as far as I knew, the main house had been in the family for several generations as well. It would be interesting to really search through the boxes at some point. I was sure there was a lot of junk, but it seemed possible there were hidden treasures as well.

"This rocking chair looks really old," Clara commented. "In fact, if I had to guess, I'd say it was homemade, not the sort of thing you could buy in a furniture store."

I glanced at the chair Clara was referring to. "I seem to remember Garrett mentioning once that his great-grandfather was a carpenter. He made that big hutch in the dining room as well as the large chest in the living room."

"Furniture that's been hand carved with love really is the best kind," Clara said.

I paused in my search when I got to a box of old documents. On the surface, it looked like it contained important papers: birth certificates, deeds, and stock certificates. I wasn't sure how much of it would still need to be kept, but I made a mental note to speak to Garrett about moving these things somewhere safer, like a safety deposit box.

"Oh, look," Clara said from across the room. "This box has photos." She held up a handful. "They look fairly old. I think the little boy standing in front of the Christmas tree must be Garrett."

I crossed the room and looked at the photos Clara had found. I picked up the one of the boy in front of the tree and took a closer look. "I do think this is Garrett. He must be four or five."

"He was such a handsome young man. Still is."

I glanced at Clara, who appeared to be blushing. Garrett and Clara? Clara was a bit older, but they were close to the same age. I'd noticed the two of them chatting at Thanksgiving, and she'd asked about him at least a half-dozen times since. I knew Clara had come to Turtle Cove to find her soul mate. Could the man she was looking for be the one who'd owned the place all along?

"I wonder if there are any photos of Frannie," I mused. "Garrett would have been three or four when she lived here, so if there are photos of him at four or five there might be some from a few years earlier."

"Do you know what she looked like?" Clara asked.

"Yes, I do. There was a photo of her in Ned's file."

I picked up a handful of photos and began to sort through them, looking for the dark-haired woman with haunted eyes and a friendly smile. The ones on the top of the box looked as if they were probably a couple of years after Frannie was murdered. It seemed someone—perhaps Garrett's mother—had been something of a photography buff; there were photos of all the important moments in Garrett's life. I realized if I looked back far enough I might even find photos of my father when he was a young man.

"Oh, look at this." Clara's eyes gleamed. "This looks like Garrett's very first Christmas. Isn't he adorable in the little red Santa suit?"

I took the photo from Clara. Not only was Garrett wearing a red suit and hat but he was being held by someone I recognized as my own father. My heart bled as I studied the look of complete fascination and adoration on the man's face. I was pretty sure my very unsentimental mother hadn't taken a single photo of me on my first Christmas, and if she'd ever had any photos of my father, she'd long since burned them. I'd have to ask Garrett if it was all right for me to make copies of whatever photos he had of the man who had fathered us both but neither of us really knew.

I continued to flip through the photos, pausing on one I was certain was of Frannie. She was sitting on a blanket on the lawn with a toddler who must have been Garrett. She had a huge smile on her face and appeared to be laughing at something the baby had said or done. Garrett said he didn't remember her, but I figured he couldn't have been more than three in this picture. I didn't think I remembered anything from that early in my life either.

I set the photo aside. Bringing along a few photos of Frannie when Jack and I conducted our interviews could help to refresh memories. I found two more of Frannie holding Garrett before coming across one that gave me pause.

"What is it, dear?" Clara asked. She must have noticed my frown.

"This photo of Frannie is different from the others. It looks like whoever took it did it without her being aware of it." I took a couple of steps toward Clara, so we were standing side by side and could look at it at the same time. "She looks so sad. One might even say haunted."

"She does appear to have something heavy on her mind," Clara agreed. "I wonder what she was looking at."

It did seem Frannie was looking at something in the distance, not at the photographer. Frannie was a beautiful woman and I could see why people might want to photograph her, but I couldn't figure out why anyone who lived at the resort would be following her around with a camera. Of course, the photo could have been taken by someone other than a Hanford, but if that were true, how did the photo get in the box?

"She almost looks frightened," Clara added. "Or nervous at the very least."

"Let's keep looking for photos of Frannie." I set the one I was holding on to the pile with the others. "I know we're supposed to be looking for Christmas decorations, but I have a feeling about these photos. I think they might provide us with a clue as to what led to Frannie's death."

"I believe you're correct." Clara nodded. "I've found photographs, especially those caught of unsuspecting subjects at random moments, to be quite informative. Like this one here." Clara held up another one.

I took the photo and looked at it. Frannie was standing on the porch of one of the cabins with her hand on the doorknob, as if she was preparing to enter. She'd paused to look over her shoulder and it seemed, based on the expression on her face, she wasn't happy about whatever or whoever she'd found behind her. "I wonder if she was being stalked."

"By whom?" Clara asked. "The fact that there are quite a few photos of Frannie that appear to capture moments when she most likely didn't realize she was being photographed might suggest a stalker, but the fact that the photos were kept here, along with Garrett's photos, indicates to me that whoever took them would most likely have been a resident of this house."

"I was just thinking the same thing. I suppose the photos could have been taken by Garrett's mother."

"Or his father. Do you know if anyone else lived here when Garrett was a baby?"

"Not as far as I know," I answered. "At least not in the main house. The resort, of course, had guests throughout the year. Let's keep looking to see if anything really pops as being a clue."

We worked side by side, going through the box a photo at a time. Photos of Frannie we set aside for further consideration; those of Garrett and others we set in another pile to be returned to the box when we were done. A lot of the photos of Frannie were posed, and most showed her with Garrett. Based on the look of adoration on her face, I thought it was safe to assume she was completely enamored with her landlord's baby and, judging by the smiles on Garrett's face, he was equally enamored with the young woman who, apparently, spent a lot of time playing with him. I wondered if seeing these photos would spark a memory in Garrett. Perhaps I'd take a few with me when Blackbeard and I visited him later in the week.

"Oh, dear," Clara said.

I paused and looked at her. If I didn't know better, I'd say she was scandalized. "What is it?"

Clara passed the photo she was looking at to me. I couldn't help but gasp as I took in the image of Frannie locked in an intimate embrace with a man whose face I couldn't see. From his hair color and body build, he could very well have been my father. "This looks like Frannie with my father."

"There are a lot of men with a similar build and coloring," Clara reminded me. "There's no way to know for certain who Frannie was with from this angle. It's apparent, however, that she was involved with someone who either lived at or was visiting the resort. I imagine that would eliminate both her husband Tom and the man who sent her the letters we found."

"While it's true we can't concretely identify the man in the photo, I wonder if the reason Garrett's mother kicked our dad off the island and out of my brother's life had more to do with an affair he was having with a young tenant than it did with his treasure hunting."

Chapter 3

Jack and I decided to have lunch at Gertie's on the Wharf. I hoped to chat with Gertie and maybe pick her brain about the photographs Clara and I had found, but the waitress informed us that Gertie had taken a trip into Charleston with the new man in her life and wouldn't be back until Thursday. Gertie was dating a retired coroner she'd recently met and I was happy she'd decided to take some time off, but I was a bit bummed she wasn't available to chat. She had a unique and usually helpful way of looking at things.

At least the restaurant wasn't crowded on this rainy Tuesday, so we managed to get a cozy table tucked into a nook where a wall of windows looked out over the marina. The rain Clara had predicted had arrived in sheets, so we decided on hot bowls of clam chowder and freshly baked bread still warm from the oven.

"I think I'm going to have to have some of whatever smells so good for dessert," I said to Jack as he studied the stack of photos I'd brought with me.

"I was just thinking the same thing. It smells like ginger cake, or maybe ginger cookies." Jack paused and looked up from the photos.

"I'm picking up a hint of pumpkin as well."

"I suppose it could be pumpkin spice bread. I guess we'll ask the waitress when she comes back." Jack looked back down at the photo in his hand. "I understand your concern about the photo, but the man with Frannie has his back to the camera. You really can't make out any of his features. Is there any particular reason you think he could be your father?"

"Not really," I admitted. "I've spent quite some time looking at the photo since Clara found it and I haven't been able to pick out a single detail that should convince me the man is Max Hanford. To be honest, from the back, he doesn't look all that much like the man I saw in the other photos of him." I reached across the table and took the photo from Jack. "This man looks to be in his twenties. That's how old Max was when he was married to Garrett's mother, and he was tall and lanky, with blond hair when he was younger. I have the photos of him and Garrett for comparison, and it's possible the man holding Garrett and the one embracing Frannie could be the same person. Of course, by the time Max met and married my mother, he was twenty years older and his hair had thinned and his waistline had thickened."

"Do you think it would do any good to show Max the photo?"

"No. Garrett's told me he's basically stopped speaking, and when he does say something, it's total gibberish. The doctor says it's doubtful he'll regain the ability to communicate."

"I'm sorry to hear that. I'd hoped you'd have more time."

"Yeah, me too, but I guess the time we did have was its own kind of miracle."

"What about showing the photo to Garrett?" Jack suggested. "I know he was very young when his father left, but maybe the photo will trigger a memory."

"I thought about doing that, but I don't want to inadvertently cause Garrett any distress. I'm hoping one of the people we speak to during our investigation will be able to shed some light on who Frannie was locking lips with."

Jack continued to thumb through the photos. "I know it appears Frannie was this young girl who loved kids and waited patiently for her husband to return from the war, but given the fact that she was married and was receiving love letters from a man who may have been her brother-in-law, and she was involved in some sort of a romantic relationship here, don't you think it's possible she wasn't the sweet thing she appeared to be?"

"The thought has crossed my mind," I said. "When we first found the letters, I got wrapped up in the romance of the whole thing. Admittedly, we don't know how Frannie felt about Paul because we only have his letters to her as an indication they even had a relationship, but the man who wrote the letters seemed to be deeply in love, so I guess I just assumed the recipient of the letters was worthy of that love. I'm less sure of that now."

"Do you want to continue with the investigation? This may be one of those cases where we find answers to questions we might end up wishing we hadn't asked."

I glanced out the window at the pouring rain as I thought about that. Things had changed for me when I'd found the photo in the attic. Garrett had loved his mother, and he'd only recently made peace with his dying father. How would he feel if he found out the reason his mother had banished his father from his life had more to do with infidelity than treasure hunting?

But I was still intrigued. It was sort of like I'd opened Pandora's box. Now that it was open, I felt an obligation to see things through.

"I guess I'd like to go on with the interviews we've set up. I'd like to leave Garrett out of this, though, until we see where they take us. I'm intrigued by the idea that Frannie may have been killed by someone who knew her, not the Strangler. I'm not sure if that's something that can be proven even if it's true, but I'm interested enough to try to find out."

"Okay; if you're in, I am too. We can reevaluate as we go and stop what we're doing at any point if we realize we're uncovering secrets best left buried."

"I agree. Plus, interviewing longtime residents about Frannie will give me an opening to slip in a few questions about Secret Santa."

"You aren't really going to pursue that idea?"

"I am. I have a major magazine interested in an article, but only if I can reveal the real hero behind the legend."

"Has it ever occurred to you that the reason Secret Santa is so secretive is because he or she doesn't want their identity revealed?"

"It has, but the person or persons who have done so many wonderful things deserve to get credit for these kind acts."

"And if they don't want it?" Jack asked.

I took a deep breath. The reporter in me wanted to care more about landing the story than keeping some random person's secret, but my time on Gull Island had softened me, and while I'd accepted the terms the magazine had insisted on, I was having second thoughts. "How about we find the person responsible for all the good deeds, and if they really don't want to be named, I'll drop the whole thing? But if they aren't adamant about not having their identity revealed, I'll have my story and they'll get the credit they deserve."

"I guess that sounds fair. But remember, the decision is theirs to make."

"Agreed."

******

By the time we finished lunch it was time to see Ned Colton. While he'd been retired for quite some time, he'd been the deputy in charge on the island when Frannie was murdered, and he seemed to have a good grasp on the overall situation.

"When we spoke last week, you indicated it was your opinion Frannie was killed by a copycat, not the Strangler himself," I began after we were seated in the dining area of the man's small home.

"That's correct. As I said, I found some anomalies that didn't add up. Unfortunately, the case wasn't mine to investigate, and the FBI concluded Mrs. Kettleman was, in fact, killed by the same monster who murdered the other girls."

"We're still trying to get a handle on exactly what happened, so maybe it would be best if you could give us an overview of what you remember about Frannie, her death, the Strangler; really anything at all," I suggested.

"I didn't know her prior to her death. From my research, I know she was staying out at the resort while her husband was overseas. By the time Mrs. Kettleman's body was found in the cemetery, the FBI was already knee deep in an investigation into whoever had killed and displayed the bodies of three other victims. While I wasn't officially involved, I spent some time looking in to things to assuage my own curiosity. My findings were less than conclusive but, I think, interesting."

"You mentioned when last we spoke that the rose left with Frannie's body had thorns, whereas the ones left with the other victims were thornless," I prompted to get him on to information we hadn't already discussed. "What other anomalies did you find?"

"There were four things other than the roses. All the women identified as victims of the Strangler were unmarried except for Mrs. Kettleman. Additionally, all the other women frequented bars and clubs and were known to leave with a different man every night. According to Mrs. Hanford, who I spoke with after Mrs. Kettleman's body was discovered, the woman who rented her cabin was a quiet woman who usually stayed in after dark. And, finally, it appeared to me that Mrs. Kettleman was hit on the head with a solid object before she was strangled. In my opinion, she was attacked and fought back. I can't know for certain, but it seemed to me the blow to the head caused her to pass out. I believe she was strangled while unconscious."

I glanced at Jack. Clara had made a point about a serial killer not being willing to deviate from his or her routine even to the smallest degree. Knocking your victim out before you killed her was a huge deviation in my book. "You said there were four things other than the rose…?"

"The mark on the women who fell victim to the Strangler. Like the other twelve women, Mrs. Kettleman bore a pentagram. Unlike the other twelve women, however, Mrs. Kettleman's was carved into her shoulder with a thin-bladed knife. The mark in the skin of the other victims had been carved by a much thicker knife."

I frowned. "That sounds significant."

"It seemed so to me as well, but when I pointed it out to the FBI agent who was conducting the investigation, he pointed out that no one other than the Strangler and law enforcement even knew about the mark. Keep in mind, Mrs. Kettleman was just the fourth victim and, at that time, the most recent. It wasn't outside the realm of possibility that something happened to the Strangler's knife of choice between victim three and four. It wasn't until later, after the data was available on all the victims, that the difference in blade became apparent."

"If Frannie was killed by a copycat, how could they have found out about the mark in the first place?" Jack asked.

"The mark was a well-guarded detail, but it's possible one of the FBI agents let it slip, maybe while having a beer with a buddy. It's also possible someone involved with the case killed Mrs.

Kettleman. Stranger things have happened. Additionally, everything was recorded on paper and kept in files back then. It's even possible one of the investigators left the file on his desk and someone—a janitor or a secretary—took a peek. Stuff gets leaked all the time. I was surprised the FBI put so much weight on that single fact."

I thought it strange as well, and I could tell by the look on Jack's face that he was beginning to have serious doubts about the validity of the initial investigation. Not only did we have the thorny rose, but Frannie had fought back and was married, even if she hadn't been faithful.

"Is there anything else that stood out to you as significant?" I asked.

"Not really. I've given considerable thought to the case, and while some of the deviations are slight, taken as a whole, I feel they're significant."

"I agree." I paused before changing the subject. "As long as we're here, is it all right if I ask you about something else?"

"Sure, I guess."

"It has to do with Secret Santa."

Ned looked surprised. "What about him?"

"I'm working on an article about his good deeds. If you look at some of the gifts, they're really amazing. My editor would like a side interview with Santa himself, but I'm having a hard time pinning down exactly who's been providing the annual Christmas miracle."

"If you're wondering if I know, I don't. The whole thing started twelve years ago, when a family lost their home in a fire. In the years since, there've been other recipients, all local people in need."

"I know the gifts vary widely from a building to house an animal shelter to a new motorized wheelchair for a man who suffered a spinal injury in an accident. Do you have any idea how Santa chooses the recipient of his annual gift?"

Ned shrugged. "No. You'd have to ask him."

"I'd like to, but I don't know who to ask. I know you said you didn't know who was providing these special gifts each year, but if you had to guess, who would you choose?"

Ned stopped to think about it. "I guess I'd have to say Evan Paddington."

"And who's he?" I asked.

"He used to be the fire chief at the local station. His father passed away fifteen or so years ago, leaving him a wealthy man. The first Secret Santa gift was made a few years later. I imagine Evan felt bad he couldn't help save the house that burned down and decided to help the family out."

"That makes sense. But why would he continue to provide Christmas miracles?"

"Maybe he realized how good giving felt."

That made perfect sense.

We thanked Ned for his time and promised to keep him up to date on our progress. Then we made a mad dash through the pouring rain to Jack's car. Our next interview was with the librarian at the time Frannie died. We'd been told Frannie was a voracious reader, so we hoped this woman would be able to tell us about her personality and personal life.

******

The library on Gull Island was small, with only a limited number of books, but it seemed to be a popular place to hang out on a rainy day and therefore was crowded when we arrived. Even though Edna Turner had long since retired, it was the library where she'd suggested we meet. After getting a look at the number of cars in the parking lot, I found myself hoping we'd be able to find a quiet place to chat.

"We're here to see Edna Turner," I said to the woman behind the counter as soon as we entered the cozy building.

"You really are Jackson Jones," the woman gasped when she looked up from the book she was checking in. "When Edna said she was meeting Jackson Jones, I thought she must be off her meds."

"I just go by Jack on the island."

"Well, just Jack, it's a real pleasure to meet you. Would you mind signing my book?"

"You have a book with you?" Jack asked.

"Actually, I do. Hang on and I'll get it."

She ran into the room behind her and returned a few minutes later with Jack's newest book. He signed it with a heart next to his name, which seemed to thrill her.

"Edna's in the back." She pointed to the doorway through which she'd returned when Jack handed her back the book. "Just follow that hallway to the end."

We thanked her and followed her directions. Edna was sitting at a long table that looked as if it were used for staff meetings and lunch breaks. Jack had spoken to her on the phone but hadn't met her in person yet, so we took a minute to introduce ourselves before jumping in with questions.

"I didn't know Frannie outside our relationship as librarian and reader, but she struck me as being quiet and introverted," Edna began. "I knew she was living at the resort and she often spoke of how cute her landlord's son was and how much she enjoyed spending time with him. I'm not sure what interests she might have had outside books, but she was a voracious reader and came in here several times a week to exchange one armload of books for another."

"Did she seem to have a reading preference?" I asked.

"Mostly romance. We had that in common. She liked a good mystery as well, and toward the end she seemed to be interested in books on childrearing. I remember thinking at the time that spending time with the Hanford boy had gotten her thinking of having a child of her own."

"Did Frannie ever talk to you about the people she spent time with?" I asked.

"Not specifically. I saw her around town with Sherry Pierce from time to time. They were about the same age and I believe they were friends. And I know she met Clint Brown for dinner at least once."

"Clint Brown. That name sounds familiar," Jack said.

"Clint still lives on the island. He used to be a real estate agent, but he's retired now, of course."

"Do you know why Frannie had dinner with him?" I asked.

"I imagine to discuss real estate. Frannie mentioned on occasion that she hoped to get her husband to agree to settle down on the island when he returned from overseas."

"Did Frannie ever mention someone named Paul?" I asked.

"No, I don't believe so. It's been a long time, but the name doesn't ring a bell."

Jack asked her about the bars, clubs, and other venues frequented by the island's young adults at the time of Frannie's death, while I tried to decide whether to ask her about Max. I definitely didn't want to make it sound as if I suspected he was cheating on his wife with Frannie, but it would be useful to know if he was still living on the island then. Finally, I asked the question.

"I can't be sure, but it seems to me that Max left right around the time Frannie was living here. I think he was gone by the time she was murdered, though I seem to remember seeing them together at the resort a time or two."

"Did you visit the resort often?" I asked.

"Not really, but I had a friend who stayed there for a long weekend every few months, and I stopped by to see her a few times while she was there."

"Is your friend still alive?" I wondered.

"No. Betsy went to be with the Lord more than twenty years ago."

I decided against showing Edna the photo of Frannie and the man embracing. She didn't seem to have known Frannie on a personal level and I hated to start a rumor even if the subject of it was long dead. If Frannie had been involved in an intimate relationship with someone on the island, chances were her good friend Sherry would have the knowledge we sought.

"Before we go, do you mind if I ask you a few questions about Secret Santa?"

Edna's entire persona softened. "There isn't a more caring person on earth. Talk about a warm heart and a genuine soul."

"So, you know who Secret Santa is?" I asked.

"Well, no, not the identity of the person who has helped out so many people in need. But I don't have to know. I can tell by the acts of kindness that a truly special soul is in our midst. Do you know, we almost lost the library six years ago? The funding had dried up, and although the staff all agreed to cut back on their paid hours and volunteer to make up the shortfall, there was a mortgage on the building we couldn't pay. Secret Santa's gift that year was to pay off our loan in full. Not only were we able to keep the library open but the staff was able to continue collecting paychecks."

"Wow," I said. "That's really something."

"It really is."

"So Secret Santa must be rich."

"Yes, I imagine he must be."

"Can you guess who it might be?"

Edna shook her head. "No, I don't, and even if I did, I wouldn't say. Secret Santa is secret for a reason, and I, for one, intend to honor the wish of this truly special person to remain anonymous. I know you newspaper types like to go digging around in every little secret, but there are some that are best left untold."

Chapter 4

"What now?" I asked Jack as we left the library and returned to his car.

"I was thinking of stopping by the seasonal store to pick up some decorations. I did a quick inventory last night and it seems I have a lot less to work with than I thought. It'll be a wet errand with the rain, however."

"That's okay. I'm already pretty wet. We can stop by the resort so I can get some dry clothes before we head to your place."

"Or," Jack countered, "we could just toss your things in the dryer once we get to my place."

"And what would I wear while I'm waiting for them to dry?" I lifted one brow.

"Preferably nothing, but I have a robe you can borrow if you prefer."

I couldn't quite prevent the heat that rose to my face. Being intimate with Jack was something I was still getting used to.

"As long as we're out and about, do you mind if I call Evan Paddington to ask if he's willing to speak to us?"

"If you must."

"I think at this point I must. I know you aren't convinced I should even be trying to unmask Secret Santa, but it's a good story I think should be told."

"I suppose that's a matter of opinion, but I respect your role as an investigative reporter, so if you want to continue the search I'm here for you."

I grinned. "Thanks. Identifying Secret Santa will make the difference in my ability to sell my story. After we meet with him we can buy the decorations, head to your house, and then decide what to do next."

Jack winked. "Sounds like a plan."

As it turned out, Evan didn't pick up when I called, so I left a message letting him know I was interested in speaking to him, and then we headed to the holiday store. The brightly lit shop was packed with people stocking up on lights, garlands, and Christmas accents, just as we were. While everything I did with Jack felt special in its own way, there was something magical about pushing baskets side by side as we walked up and down each aisle, selecting the perfect decorations for both his house and the one at the resort. I hadn't had a lot of relationships that lent themselves to everyday tasks like shopping and decorating, and for the first time it struck me just how much fun I'd been missing out on.

"White or colored?" Jack held up two packs of Christmas lights.

"For?" I asked.

"The tree."

"While either would look nice, personally, I think white lights with colorful ornaments would look beautiful."

"White it is." Jack tossed several boxes of lights into his basket. "I figured I'd bring my truck to the tree lot when we do our shift tomorrow. We can get trees for my house and yours. If you want, I can stay to help you get the lights on your tree. Then you can add the ornaments at your leisure."

"Thanks. I appreciate that." I tossed several boxes of white lights into my basket, just in case. I'd never gotten around to figuring out what Garrett had packed away, but I figured I could use the lights to decorate my room if he had the tree covered. "Putting the lights on will be the hardest part. I thought I'd see if Clara and Victoria wanted to help with the actual decorating. I know Brit's busy and I doubt the guys will want to do it."

"I wouldn't count George out until you ask him," Jack counseled. "He seems exactly the sort to enjoy a good old-fashioned decorating party."

Jack had a point. George probably would enjoy sipping eggnog while we listened to carols and put ornaments on the tree.

We got everything we needed for the trees, then headed to the aisle of tabletop décor. I wanted to get some items for my room as well as a centerpiece for the dining table and something for the mantel. By the time we'd found everything we needed I was starving. We'd both dried off while we shopped, so we decided to head to the pizza place to pick up a pie to take back to Jack's house. We planned to get started on the Christmasization of his home after we ate.

The pizza place was festively decorated, much like the rest of the island. As soon as we walked in, I noticed George sitting at a table with Meg Collins, who volunteered at the museum. The two of them had been dating casually for a couple of weeks. George waved us over, so I tapped Jack on the shoulder and nodded in their direction.

"Would you like to join us?" George asked.

"We're just here to pick up some takeout." I glanced at the clock. "We called it in, so it should be ready in about five minutes, although it's so crowded today, it might take a while longer."

"I think a fair number of holiday shoppers decided to pop in for pizza once the rain started back up," George commented. "Meg and I were lucky to get a table."

"It's so warm and cozy in here, I don't blame people for congregating during the storm." I glanced at Jack. "We don't want to interrupt you."

"Nonsense; have a seat until your order is ready," Meg invited. "George was just telling me about the interesting case your group has become involved in."

"It does seem to be an interesting if not somewhat complicated case," I responded.

"I uncovered something that may be relevant," George said.

I looked at Jack, who nodded. We both slid into the booth.

"What did you find out?" I asked, intrigued by George's comment.

"I came across an article written by a man named Sam Ringer in 1969. It was published in a small-press magazine that dealt with conspiracy theories and unsolved mysteries and discussed some short stories by a writer using the name Henry Post. It seemed he published one story a month for twelve months in 1965 and 1966. The interesting thing about the series was that the plot of each story mirrored one of the killings credited to the Silk Stocking Strangler."

I raised a brow. "So, the stories were published after the Strangler stopped killing. Maybe the author was familiar with the murders."

"Perhaps," George agreed. "But Sam Ringer, the man who wrote the 1969 article, made an argument that the reason the details in the short stories were so accurate was because Henry Post was the Strangler."

"Seems risky to publish stories that detail murders you committed just a year after you ended the killing spree," I pointed out.

"True. But in Ringer's article, he suggested Henry was careful, and although he tried to track him down, he was never able to put a real name to the one the writer had used."

"If he wrote twelve stories about twelve murders, was Frannie's included? If it wasn't, that could be a clue that she really wasn't a Strangler victim," I realized.

"I am trying to track down the stories themselves to see if Frannie's is among them," George confirmed. "The magazine that published them is out of business, but I am hoping I can find digital copies."

"If Henry and the Strangler are in fact the same person, and Henry wrote the stories after the last death was discovered, it would mean he intentionally stopped killing and wasn't killed or jailed on another charge," Jack said. "Why would he?"

"Ringer believed the Strangler intended to kill twelve women all along. He suggested the pentagram the Strangler carved on the shoulders of his victims was proof of it. It seems the pentagram was modified in such a way that there were twelve points if you counted the ones directed both inward and outward from the center. It's Ringer's theory the Strangler had a predetermined plan, and when he finished his task, he decided to share his story with the world."

"You'd think the feds would have been all over that," I said.

"Maybe, but Henry did publish his stories in a small press, and back in the sixties we didn't have the internet to spread things on a global scale the way we do now. I'm not sure Ringer's theory holds water, but he made a good enough case that I am very interested in looking in to things a bit more."

Jack got up when his name was called from the takeout window.

"It sounds like you might be on to something." I stood up as well. "Let us know what you find." I turned to Meg. "Oh, and I want to chat with you about an article I'm working on. Will you be at the museum tomorrow morning?"

"After ten."

"I'll stop by after my visit with Garrett."

We picked up the pizza and headed to Jack's house. It was still pouring, so he gave me a robe to slip into while he changed his clothes and tossed mine in the dryer. As soon as we were dry and warm, he opened a bottle of wine and we enjoyed the cheesy pie, which we'd ordered piled high with toppings.

"This is really nice," I said as I listened to the rain hitting a nearby window while the reflection of the fire flickered on the glass. I was excited to help Jack decorate his home, though by this point a large part of me just wanted to relax and watch it rain.

"I need to dig out my Christmas CDs," Jack said.

"You have Christmas CDs?" I had to admit I was surprised.

"I have a couple. I probably shouldn't tell you this, but an old girlfriend brought them over and never came back for them after I told her I was going to Cabo rather than spending the holiday with her."

"Ouch."

Jack shrugged. "I guess I was a bit of a jerk back then, but that was the old me. New me wants nothing more than to spend the holiday with you."

I tried to offer a sincere smile, although the thought of Jack with another woman wasn't sitting well with me. Of course, I knew there were women in his past; a lot of them. I just preferred not to dwell on them if I could avoid it.

"What did you think about George's serial-killer-turned-author theory?" I asked, changing the subject.

"I'd be amazed if it turned out to be true, but if it did, I guess it would confirm there were twelve and not thirteen victims. I suppose the only way to prove Frannie wasn't killed by the Strangler would be to read the twelve stories to see if she's included. Would you like more wine?"

I pushed my glass toward Jack in a gesture of acceptance. "It seems the storm is getting worse."

"Maybe you should stay over tonight," Jack suggested. "I can take you home in the morning."

"I don't have my things. Not even a toothbrush."

"I have an extra toothbrush and a T-shirt you can sleep in," Jack offered.

It was very cozy in his home and I had no desire to go back out into the storm, but that felt like a big step. Jack and I had never spent the whole night together, although he was planning to stay at the resort on Christmas. "I'll need to call Clara to ask her to tuck Blackbeard in for the night, but I'm sure that won't be a problem."

Jack smiled. "It's settled, then. I've been thinking you might want to bring some stuff over here. Stuff you can leave for nights like this, when you decide to stay."

I nodded but didn't reply. I felt as if I needed to think about that for a bit, but in the end, I suspected I'd do as Jack suggested. Once Garrett moved back to the house and was there to take care of Blackbeard, he wouldn't be a consideration. I was sure Garrett would need a certain amount of help, so I'd have to see how things worked out.

"Your clothes should be dry. I'll grab them and then we can begin draping lights."

I had a feeling Jack had just given me the minute I needed, and for that I was grateful. I really was happy our relationship was maturing and progressing, but when it came to love I tended to be cautious. I liked to take baby steps along the way.

I grabbed my phone to call Clara. I noticed I had a missed call and a voicemail when I logged on. I clicked over to listen to the voicemail.

"Jillian, it's Margo Bronson. I have an opportunity to discuss with you that I'm sure you'll find too good to pass up…."

I listened as Margo explained that she had just taken over as managing director for the second-largest news magazine in the country and was on a mission to conquer the number-one spot. She'd done some housecleaning and had brought in some fresh talent. She wanted me on her team and was offering me not only a way back into my old life, but one with a considerable raise.

"Something wrong?" Jack asked when he returned to the room.

"No. I had a voicemail from an old friend." I wasn't sure why I didn't elaborate, but I knew I needed to think about Margo's offer before I brought Jack or anyone else into the mix. "I was just going to call Clara. If she can see to Blackbeard and you'll take me home first thing in the morning, I'd like to stay."

Jack's grin and the very lengthy kiss that followed managed to chase all thoughts of job offers and a New York lifestyle out of my mind. At least until the following day, when the offer would become all that much more real.

Chapter 5

Wednesday, December 13

As soon as Jack dropped me off at the resort, I grabbed a quick shower, changed my clothes, and tried to work up the courage to return Margo's call. A few months ago, I would have been over-the-moon happy to receive such an offer, but now? Now, I wasn't quite as certain. The job Margo was offering really was a dream come true. I'd never managed to get any momentum going on the book I kept saying I was going to write, so in a way, my career as a journalist had morphed into a job as a glorified innkeeper.

Margo was offering me the chance to make my mark on the national scene. She was not only talking about giving me my old life back but an upgraded version of it. I didn't see how I could turn her down, yet I found myself hesitating. At the least, I owed her a return call, so I dialed her number and waited.

"Jillian, how are you, dear?" Margo asked.

"I'm good. And wow: managing director. Congratulations."

"Thank you, dear. I'm completely energized by this opportunity and, as you used to say, ready to conquer the world. From the moment I accepted the position I knew I needed to have you on my team. So, when can you start?"

I paused. "Your offer is a dream come true and you know I'd love to work with you again, but my life is a bit more complicated than when we last spoke. I have a resort to run and a brother who needs me. I guess what I'm trying to say is that while I'm very interested in your offer, I need some time to think it through before I make a decision."

"You need to think it over? I thought you'd be thrilled."

"I am thrilled, but as I said, things are complicated. Can I give you my answer next week?"

Margo didn't answer right away. I suspected she was going to move on to someone else if I wasn't willing to commit at that moment, but after a few seconds she agreed to let me get back to her on Monday. She said she really hoped I'd be able to start when they returned to work after Christmas break and asked me to give her offer the consideration it deserved, and I agreed to do so.

I loaded Blackbeard into his travel carrier for the trip to the assisted living facility where Garrett lived. What I'd really have preferred to do was take a long walk to think things through, but it was important for both bird and brother to have regular visits, so I tried to make sure they saw each other at least once a week.

"*Captain Jack, Captain Jack,*" Blackbeard said when we arrived.

"That *is* Captain Jack." I watched as Jack kissed an older woman on the cheek and then headed in my direction. "I wasn't expecting to see you here," I said as he approached and kissed me too.

"I got a call from a friend after I dropped you off. We're working on a project together and she wanted to discuss a few things with me."

"A friend?"

"Valerie McCall. She's a writer as well. Perhaps you've heard of her."

I looked toward the woman, who was sitting in a chair on the outdoor patio with a throw over her legs. "That's Valerie McCall? I love her books. I read every one of the books in her Pippy Porter PI series when I was a kid. I think those books made me fall in love with reading, which led to a love of writing."

"You should tell her that. I'm sure it'll make her day."

"I will. Thanks." I kissed Jack's check and he continued toward the parking lot while I went on to the patio, where I'd arranged to meet Garrett, who hadn't arrived yet.

"Ms. McCall," I said as I walked up to her with Blackbeard on my shoulder.

"Oh, what a beautiful bird."

"His name is Blackbeard. He belongs to my brother, Garrett."

"You must be Jill." She smiled. "I've heard so much about you from Jack and Garrett. It's lovely to meet you."

I placed Blackbeard on the perch I'd brought for him and sat down across from the woman, who looked a lot older than the photo on her book jackets. While the facility didn't allow pets inside, they did have a nice patio and lawn where leashed pets were welcome. The patio was covered and provided outdoor heaters in the winter, so unless the island was experiencing a wind/rain event such as the one yesterday, it was usually a perfectly comfortable place to visit.

"I'm honored to meet you. I just told Jack that I read every single one of your Pippy Porter PI books when I was growing up. The books not only created a lifelong love of reading but an interest in investigation. I probably owe my entire life's path to you."

Her smile deepened. "It's so good to hear that. I haven't published for quite a few years now. At times, it's hard to remember my work amounted to something."

"Oh, it did. Your books are wonderful." I glanced at the door leading inside and still didn't see Garrett, so I continued the conversation. "How do you know Jack?"

"Our publisher introduced us a whole lotta years ago. Jack was working on his fourth or fifth book then, and he seemed to have hit a wall. My editor asked if I'd be willing to meet with one of their young writers and perhaps offer some counsel, and I agreed. Jack and I hit it off right away, even though he wasn't yet twenty-five and I was already well into my fifties. I could see immediately that his main problem was the distractions in his life, so I offered him the use of the cabin I had here on Gull Island. I figured the only way he was going to get any work done was if he had a quiet writing retreat. He took me up on my offer and finished the book in record time. After that, he began to use the cabin to work on his novels during the times he felt he needed to escape from the world."

"What a fantastic story. I had no idea Jack had been coming to the island for so long."

"The cabin was destroyed more than a decade ago, but Jack had grown to love the area, so eventually, he bought the newspaper and the house he now lives in. I had a stroke eight years ago and decided to retire here. Colin and the others have been wonderful."

"*Man overboard, man overboard*," Blackbeard said, as he always did when he saw Garrett. I looked up as he wheeled himself out the door.

I turned back to Valerie. "I should go, but it was so nice to meet you."

"It was nice to meet you as well, dear."

As soon as Garrett got close enough, Blackbeard flew to him, landed on his shoulder, and gave him a kiss on the cheek.

"It's good to see you," Garrett said.

I followed Blackbeard's lead and kissed Garrett on the cheek before taking a seat on a patio chair across from him. I noticed Valerie had gone in after Garrett came out.

"I'm sorry I'm late," Garrett said. "I got tied up in physical therapy."

"It's not a problem. I had a lovely chat with Valerie McCall. I had no idea she lived here."

"Has for years. She's a very nice woman and a writer. I guess it should have occurred to me to introduce you."

"I read her books when I was a child. I think she's the reason I love investigating so much."

"Then I'm glad my being late worked out."

I smiled. "Before we get to talking about something else and I forget to confirm things, let's talk about Christmas."

"*Ho, ho, ho,*" Blackbeard said.

I grinned at the bird before I continued. "Brit's in a play next week. We're all planning to see it on Friday evening and I'd love it if you could come with us."

"I'd like that. It's been a while since I've been to the community theater, but I used to attend quite often. When will you pick me up?"

"Following the play, we're having a writers' retreat dinner before Alex takes off for the Bahamas, so I thought it would make the most sense for us to pick you up Thursday afternoon and get you settled in at the resort. That way you'll be rested up for the play. Will that work for you?"

"I think that will be fine. I made arrangements to be away from here until January 2, although if things don't go well for some reason, I can come back at any time."

"Things are going to be fantastic," I said firmly. "Jack has finished the renovations, including the modification to the shower and sink in your private bath. We even installed a cage for Blackbeard in your room so he can hang out with you. The doorways on the first floor have all been widened and the ramps into the house were already in place when you visited on Thanksgiving." I paused. "I know this is a big step for you, but the resort is your home. There are a whole lot of people who love you and want to do whatever it takes to make sure you're comfortable."

"And I appreciate that. I'm doing better and can get around fairly well on my own, so I hope I won't need a lot of assistance. I've even had some sessions using a walker. My therapist thinks I might be out of this wheelchair for good in a few months if I work hard and do my exercises every day."

"That's fantastic news."

"I'm happy with my progress. Will it just be us for Christmas?"

"Actually, it will be us and Jack and Clara. Everyone else is leaving for a couple of days, but I suspect the four of us will have a wonderful Christmas Eve and Christmas Day."

"I'm looking forward to it. I found Clara to be witty and interesting when I met her at Thanksgiving, and I've always liked Jack."

"Clara, Vikki, and I are planning to decorate the resort. I know you have some decorations that used to be in the attic. I bought some too, but I wanted to know if there was anything specific you wanted to be sure we dug out."

"Are you doing a tree?"

"Yes."

"Then I'd love to see my grandmother's Christmas angel on the top. It should be in the same box as the other decorations."

"I'll look for it this evening. Did you and your mother share any special traditions?"

"I'm not sure I'd call them traditions, but I have some fond memories. My mother was first and foremost a businesswoman. She owned and ran the resort, so her business was being a host. And she was a good one. Every year she'd hire a crew from town to come out to decorate the entire resort. It was magical. They strung lights in some of the smaller trees, and every cabin door had a bright green wreath with an even brighter red ribbon."

"It sounds nice."

"It was. Mom even hired a horse-drawn wagon to entertain the guests. They decorated that as well, and then took wagonloads of people on rides around the island. And there was caroling and hot cocoa to drink."

I could just imagine the fun that must have been.

"And, of course, there was Christmas Eve dinner. The resort was always filled to capacity over Christmas. Mom worked a lot of hours, and although she hired help from town, I was usually handed off to a babysitter for most of the two-week holiday period. Still, on Christmas Eve Mom had a special dinner for all the guests. She hired men who moved out all the furniture from the rooms downstairs and then brought in a long table and covered it with bright red tablecloths. Invitations to Christmas Eve dinner at the resort was much sought after. We usually had the place booked a year in advance."

"It really does sound magical," I said. "And it does sound as if you did grow up with traditions."

"Maybe. At the time I was mostly just irritated that I had to spend the whole Christmas holiday with a babysitter. But Mom and I did have Christmas together. After dinner on Christmas Eve she'd have the furniture brought back in and the two of us would put on Christmas carols on the hi-fi and open gifts. We'd watch an old movie on TV, then curl up on the sofa with a warm blanket. More often than not, Mom would be so exhausted she'd fall asleep there, so I'd curl up with her and we'd both be there all night. By the time breakfast rolled around the next morning, Mom would be busy again, but we did have those few hours together on Christmas Eve."

I reached over and put my arm around Garrett. "I think I'm going to cry. I know having your mom busy was hard on you, but at least you had those few hours. My own mother usually went to a party on Christmas Eve and slept in Christmas morning. She took me to brunch on Christmas Day, but one or more of her friends would come along."

"Sounds lonely."

I glanced at Garrett. "It was. But enough about that. Let's get back to decorations. I started to look for the stuff yesterday but got distracted by a box of photos."

"Oh?"

I pulled a couple I'd selected out of my bag. "I found a whole boxful. This one is of you and our dad on your first Christmas." I passed it to Garrett.

"I can't remember us ever being happy as a family, but we do look happy here."

"You do. I was wondering if you minded if I made a copy. I don't have any photos of our father."

"Please, feel free to make copies of anything you want, although I'm surprised your mother didn't take any photos of their time together."

"Mom isn't the sentimental sort. She has a ton of photos of herself that are plastered all over social media, but she never really took pictures of other people. She wasn't happy when Dad left, so I suspect if she ever had any photos, she destroyed them."

"I suppose that's understandable. I'm afraid our father never stuck around long."

I showed him a couple more photos of him and our dad. "You really were a cute baby."

Garrett smiled. "I was, wasn't I?"

"I couldn't find any photos of your mother. Not that I looked extensively, but I did find it odd."

"Unlike your mother, who likes to have photos taken of herself, my mom didn't like to pose. Besides, Mom was the photographer in our family. She was a busy woman, but she could oftentimes be found wandering around the resort, snapping photos. I'm sure there are several boxes of photos of wildlife stashed away somewhere."

"I'd love to see them. I'll have to take a closer look in the storage room when I have some time."

"There was a lot of junk up in the attic, but I'm sure you'll find some interesting things as well. I kept planning to sort through all that stuff, but I never did. I guess I never will, now that I can't climb up to the second floor."

"Maybe we can look in to installing a lift." I shuffled the photos and selected another one. "I know you said you didn't remember Frannie, the woman whose death we're investigating, but I found this photo of the two of you." I passed it to Garrett.

He looked at it, smiled, then frowned. "She does seem familiar, but I was so young when she stayed with us, I can't remember anything specific. How's the investigation going?"

I narrowed my eyes. "I think we're on the way to demonstrating that Frannie wasn't one of the Silk Stocking Strangler's victims, but we don't have any firm leads to who may have really killed her. There's a possibility it was her husband, Tom. She died just five days after he got home from Vietnam, and there's a fair amount of evidence to support the idea that she may have been unfaithful to him."

"I guess jealousy is as good a motive as any for murder."

"Jack and I have some interviews set up for this afternoon, and George is working on the theory that the Stalker himself may have fictionalized and published the details of his killing spree. If he did, and George can find the stories, we should be able to confirm whether Frannie was a victim."

"There are many reasons I'm anxious to move home, but joining your Mastermind group ranks at the top. There are only so many books you can read and so many television shows you can watch before complete and total boredom sets in."

I could imagine how boring it would be to have to look at the same four walls day in and day out. There would be challenges in bringing Garrett home for good, but I was committed to it, and the other writers were as well. One way or another, we'd make it happen. Of course, once he moved home, if he really was able to use a walker, he really wouldn't need me to run the place for him. The timing of his announcement combined with my job offer wasn't lost on me. Sure, Garrett would probably always need some help, but he could hire a manager and oversee the work himself, and I had a gut feeling Clara would be willing to help him with cooking and other personal tasks. Was the job in New York my destiny? It would put me in a position to make a real impact in national news. Funny, I wasn't more excited by that thought.

"Listen, before I go, I wanted to ask you about Secret Santa."

"What about him?"

"I'm working on an article on the fantastic gifts Secret Santa has bestowed on people in the community over the years and would love to get a quote from the man himself. The problem is, I don't know who Secret Santa is. Any ideas?"

"I have a few ideas, but I have a feeling Secret Santa won't want to be interviewed."

"If I track him or her down and they don't want to be interviewed, I'll respect their wishes. I just figured it would be nice for this fantastic person to get the credit they deserve."

Garrett frowned but eventually responded. "I guess if I were you, I'd speak to Colin Walton."

"The man who owns this facility?"

"Colin's a good man with a generous heart. He never turns anyone away because of an inability to pay. I don't know if he has the financial resources to do everything Secret Santa has done, but he seems to be financially secure."

"Okay; thanks. I'll stop at the desk on my way out to make an appointment with him."

******

I left a message for Colin Walton to call me, then headed to the museum to speak to Meg. She'd lived on the island a long time and knew a lot of people. Evan Paddington had never called me back and I still needed to follow up with the first lead I'd jotted down with my pink pen, a woman named Vera Stone. Hopefully, one of them would be the Santa I was looking for and I'd have my story and could turn all my attention to Frannie.

"Thank you for meeting with me," I said to Meg as I entered the museum with Blackbeard on my shoulder.

"I'm always happy to help you when I can. You and your friends have been so nice to include me in your activities."

"We're all happy to include you. The reason I'm here today is to ask about Secret Santa."

"Secret Santa?"

"I'm writing an article about the man or woman behind the legend and would love to arrange for an interview. The problem is, I don't know who Secret Santa is."

"I see. And you think I might know?"

"I hoped you did. So far, I have a few leads but nothing concrete."

Meg tilted her head slightly to the left, away from my eyes, before responding. "Who do you have on your list?"

"Evan Paddington, Vera Stone, and Colin Walton."

Meg tapped her chin with a finger. "While Colin is a very generous man, I doubt it's him. He seems to have found his niche by providing health care and housing to the elderly regardless of their ability to pay. He's a savvy businessman who's done well for himself, but my sense is that he puts any extra money he comes across into upgrading his equipment and making additions to the senior facility."

That made sense. Colin probably wasn't my man.

"Vera Stone is undoubtedly a very wealthy woman. She serves on several charitable boards and is well known for her generous donations. But Vera is

Jewish, so it seems unlikely she would use the Santa legend to help those in need."

Another good point. Which left me with just one possibility.

"Evan is a wonderful man. He inherited some money that would have allowed him to retire early, but he wanted to serve the community, so he continued to fight fires until the regular age. The first Christmas miracle, as we refer to the donations, did occur as the result of a house fire. I would say he's your best candidate of the three."

"Can you think of anyone else I didn't mention?"

"No one comes to mind right off, but I'll call you if someone does."

******

By the time I got back to the resort it was almost time to meet Jack, but Vikki, Clara, Alex, Brit, and George had all pitched in to begin the transformation of the resort into a Christmas wonderland.

"Wow. It looks so beautiful."

"We put lights on all the occupied cabins except for Nicole's," Brit informed me. "I knocked on her door and asked if she'd like lights, but she just glared at me, so I left."

Nicole was our newest resident. She was quiet and kept to herself, so she wasn't a bother, but she'd made it clear she didn't want to be disturbed, and she sometimes lashed out at anyone who dared to try to include her in group activities.

"She'll come around," Clara assured us all. "Sometimes these things take time."

I hoped Clara was right. I could sense Nicole had suffered some huge tragedy in her life that had caused her to pull away from people, but the others in the writers' retreat were a close-knit group who would welcome and embrace her if only she'd let them.

"Alex and I are going to string white lights over the top of the pergola," Brit said. "It'll be fun to sit outside after dark on the warmer nights with the lights twinkling overhead. Uncle George ordered an outdoor fireplace that should be here by tomorrow. All we need is to buy some wood and we'll be toasty warm."

"Speaking of toasty," Clara added, "if we're going to have an outdoor fire we really should have marshmallows to roast. It's been years, but there was a time when toasting a mallow to golden brown was one of my favorite summertime activities."

I could just picture the outdoor deck lit up like a Christmas tree. It would be fun to sit around the fire and tell stories as long as the weather held. We could bundle up against the cold, but if the rain returned, there wasn't a lot we could do about it.

"Jack and I are going to pick up a tree when we're at the lot this afternoon. I thought we could decorate it either tonight or tomorrow morning. Jack volunteered to stay tonight to deal with the lights."

Clara clapped her hands together. "Agatha and I are over the moon with excitement."

I grinned. "Yeah, me too. Let's go grab the boxes of decorations Garrett has stored while I have so much willing help. We can just stack them in the living room and go through them at our leisure. Garrett said to use what we want and skip what we don't. His only request was that his grandmother's Christmas angel be placed atop the tree."

"Did you ask Garrett about the photos?" Clara asked.

"What photos?" Brit inquired.

"Clara and I found a box of photos yesterday. Some of them were of Frannie when she stayed here. There was one of her locked in an intimate embrace with a man." I looked at Clara. "And no, I didn't ask Garrett about that one."

"Woo-wee, that girl sure got around," Brit said. I had to smile; *woo-wee* was completely out of character for the young woman.

I nodded. "Between the love letters we found and the photo, I have to agree."

"Do you think that's what could have led to her death?" Alex asked. "Personally, I like a woman who's free with her affections, but there are a lot of guys with a jealous streak."

"I thought of that. At this point we can't really know, but it does seem as if jealousy could be a motive if it turns out her murder was personal and not part of some madman's killing spree."

"If her murder was personal, her killer must have been someone in law enforcement," Brit said. "Are we sure we want to be digging around in a case where the bad guy might end up being a dirty cop?"

"Given the circumstances, we should proceed with caution. I certainly don't want to arouse the attention of the wrong person. Ned did point out that the killer didn't necessarily have to be a cop, just someone who had access to the same information the FBI did. It could even have been a secretary or a janitor who came across a file that was left out on a desk."

"I guess that's true," Brit agreed.

"Besides, chances are the killer, if still alive, would be in his or her midseventies at least. Even if they were dangerous at one time, it doesn't mean they still would be now."

"I can see how challenging researching such an old case is," Brit agreed. "One of the guys in the play told me that his grandfather, who just turned ninety, has lived on the island for his entire life. I didn't bring up Frannie or the case, but I did express interest in chatting at some point with a man who'd lived through so much and had such a rich history to share. Brandon assured me that his grandfather loved to share old stories, and he was sure he would be willing to chat with me. He's going to try to set something up for later in the week. If I have the opportunity to speak to him, I'll do my best to work Frannie and her murder into the conversation."

"Thanks, Brit; that would be very helpful." I glanced at my watch. "Let's go grab those boxes before Jack gets here. It'll be nice to have everything ready to go on the tree once the lights are up."

"I think I'll make some ginger cake," Clara announced. "You have to have a sweet to nibble when you decorate for the holiday."

"I really miss my mom's sugar cookies," Brit said softly.

"Then we'll make them as well. My mom always baked up a storm when the holidays rolled around. It seems this year might be a good time to revisit some of the old traditions."

"My favorites are those little round cookies with powdered sugar," Alex contributed. "My mom called them snowball cookies."

"I know just the ones you mean," Clara assured him. "I can whip up a batch of those, and maybe some fudge. My mama made the best fudge."

After we brought down the boxes, Clara and the others headed to the kitchen and I pulled Vikki aside. "You'll never guess who called me."

"Who?" Vikki asked.

"Margo Bronson."

Vikki frowned.

"She took over as managing director for one of the biggest news magazines in the country and offered me a job. A good one, with a substantial raise over what I used to make."

"Are you going back to New York?"

I blew out a breath. "I don't know. I told her I needed a few days to think about it and she gave me until Monday. I'm really conflicted. I love my life here, but what she's offering is a dream job. Not only would it allow me to return to the life I once valued very much but I'd be returning to journalism in a position of influence and respect."

"Wow." Vikki gave me a hug. "I think I might cry."

"Don't cry. I haven't decided for sure what I'm going to do yet. And please don't mention this to anyone else. I don't want to even bring it up unless I decide to take the job. I'm aware that my leaving will affect a lot of people and I promise I'll be taking that into consideration."

Vikki squeezed my hand. "I know you will. It's an important decision. I won't say a word, but if you need to talk I'm here for you."

"Thanks. I appreciate that."

By the time Jack came by to pick me up for our afternoon of sleuthing and tree selling, Clara had started her first batch of cookies and the decorations from the storage room had been sorted in anticipation of the tree. Vikki was working on the mantel and Brit was weaving a colorful garland for the stair railing. I wished I had time to stay home to help, but Jack and I had a killer to identify. For the moment, Christmas would have to wait.

Chapter 6

Sherry Pierce had been a friend of Frannie's during the time she'd lived on Gull Island. Now in her seventies, she was a widow who owned a small house a block from the water. Before she retired, she'd worked as a teacher and seemed to know a lot of people on the island. I hoped she would have the insight we needed to figure out what had been going on in Frannie's life at the time she was killed. I also hoped she would be able to verify who Paul was.

Sherry was standing on her front porch when Jack and I pulled up in front of her pretty yellow house. She waved at us as we got out of his truck. She looked as if she might have been about to set out for a jog. Not only was she wearing a yellow sweat suit but she had bright blue Nike's on her feet.

"Did we come at a bad time?" I asked as we joined her.

"Not if you don't mind a walk. I do three miles a day every day the weather cooperates. It's good for the heart, and the mind as well."

I glanced at Jack. He shrugged. "Okay," I said. "I guess it would be nice to walk and talk."

"Excellent." Sherry set off at a brisk pace. "You mentioned on the phone that you wanted to speak to me about Frannie Kettleman. What is it you'd like to know?"

"Jack and I are looking in to the possibility that Frannie wasn't killed by the Strangler, as most people believe, but by someone she knew. I've been told the two of you were friends and hoped you might be able to provide some insight into what was going on in her life in the weeks prior to her death. If she was killed by someone she knew, we're hoping we'll be able to figure out what precipitated her death."

"Before I answer, may I ask why you believe she was killed by someone other than the Strangler?" Sherry asked as she left the pavement and headed down a dirt trail toward the white sand beach this part of the island was famous for.

"There were some inconsistencies in her death when compared to the other twelve victims," I answered, trying to keep up with her without huffing and puffing. "We don't know for certain that the Strangler didn't kill Frannie, but we want to at least look at other possibilities. It seems to us that very few, if any, suspects other than the Strangler were even considered during the investigation."

"I agree the investigation seemed to be singularly focused," Sherry admitted as the dirt trail gave way to hard-packed sand. "And I've often wondered myself if attributing her death to the Strangler wasn't just an easy way to close the case." She stopped walking and looked out at the gently rolling waves. "I'd like to help you, but I'm hesitant to bring up matters that are probably left buried."

"What matters?" I asked.

Sherry had a look of contemplation on her face that seemed to indicate she was thinking things over very carefully before speaking. "Frannie wasn't a virtuous woman. Not that she was a bad person, but she seemed to take her vow of fidelity in marriage as something of a suggestion rather than an ironclad promise. I know of at least three men she had relationships with during her stay on Gull Island. And all the while, she was married to a long-suffering man who was risking his life in Vietnam."

I found it odd that she had been Frannie's friend when she seemed to have had such a low regard for the way she lived her life. I wanted to ask about that but decided to wait and let Sherry continue at her own pace.

She started walking again before she continued. "When I first met Frannie, I was drawn to her energy and enthusiasm. I admired the fact that although her young husband had been drafted, and despite the hardship I was certain she'd been forced to bear, she always greeted me with a huge smile on her face and a cheerful demeanor. It wasn't until we'd been friends for six months or so that my opinion of her started to change."

"And why did it change?" I asked.

"I happened to see her entering a motel room with a man I knew was both married and expecting a child. It seemed obvious based on their body language that they were on the verge of becoming intimate. I knew the man's wife quite well, so I knocked on the door, pulled Frannie outside, and asked her what she was doing. She laughed and reminded me that her husband had been away for a long time, and a young woman had needs. I reminded her that the man with whom she was about to satisfy her needs was married, with a baby on the way. Frannie just shrugged, said the man's wife was very pregnant, and man had needs as well. She gave me a hug, promised to catch up with me the next day, and then returned to the sinner who was waiting inside."

Sherry paused and took a deep breath. "I wanted to be mad at Frannie—in fact, I was quite outraged at first—but if you knew her, you would know she wasn't the sort it was easy to stay mad at. She told me that she was sorry I was upset and her afternoon tryst was a onetime thing; she had no plans to see the man again. Eventually, I let it go and we returned to being almost inseparable."

"Are you willing to share the name of that man?" I asked.

"I am not. I'm afraid talk of his indiscretion could affect his current relationships, even so many years later. I have no reason to believe he killed Frannie."

"All right. What about the other two men?"

"The next man Frannie admitted to sharing a bed with was Roland Carver, who was single at the time. He is and was quite a womanizer. I doubt he'd care if I still think it's wrong that a married woman should be carrying on the way she was. Still, it didn't appear anyone had gotten hurt by that fling, which lasted a few weeks at the most. I never knew the identity of the third man."

"How do you know there even was a third man?" I asked as Sherry climbed up onto a small bluff that looked out over the sea.

"Because three weeks before she died, Frannie told me that she was pregnant. She wasn't far enough along for the baby to have belonged to either of the men I knew about, so I could only surmise there had been a third man."

I glanced at Jack, who frowned.

"So Frannie was pregnant when she died?" I asked.

"I guess she must have been. She wasn't showing yet and I have no way of knowing whether she planned to keep the baby, but my instinct was that she hadn't had an abortion."

"Do you think she was considering one?" I asked.

"Perhaps. I know she was concerned about the fact that her husband was coming home. She mentioned several times that she wasn't ready and had thought she'd have more time."

"Time for what?" I asked.

"I don't know. She didn't say specifically, but I imagine it had to do with the baby. The last time I saw her was three days before her body was found. He husband had been home for a couple of days and she admitted to me that marrying him had been a mistake. She seemed to be frightened and appeared to want a way out. She told me she was working on a plan to extricate herself from the mess she was in. I never saw her again."

"Do you think her husband killed her?"

"I think he might have."

"Did Frannie ever mention a man named Paul to you?" Jack asked.

Sherry shook her head. "No. It doesn't ring a bell." Sherry stopped walking and looked out over the sea. The harbor was visible in the distance. "I just love this spot. Of all the locations on the island, this is where I feel the closest to my husband. We used to come up here and watch the fishing boats come in. We liked to make up stories about the men who worked the boats and the bounty they hauled in, day after day."

"That's nice," I said.

"Sometimes I feel all I have left of him are my memories. I spend time each day with them to make sure they don't fade away."

"Did you have children?"

"No. We were unable to conceive. I wished for children for many years but now, looking back, I can see what I had with Gary was perfect." Sherry glanced at me. "I can't explain why Frannie made the decisions she did, but I believe deep down inside she was a lonely woman who found herself married to a man she feared. She didn't deserve to die the way she did. I hope you figure out who ended her life before it really had had the chance to begin."

Sherry held a hand to her heart and then blew a kiss out toward the ocean, turned, and began to retrace her steps. I knew I probably should ask additional questions about Frannie's murder and about Secret Santa, but my instinct told me enough had been said, at least for today. When we returned to Sherry's house, we thanked her and said good-bye, then headed to our appointment with ex-Mayor Roland Carver, one of the three men Sheryl told us Frannie had been sleeping with.

******

Carver was a tall, thin man with faded blue eyes and a full head of white hair. He'd been the mayor of Gull Island at the time of Frannie's death but had long since retired. Based on the information Jack had dug up, he was eighty-three, had never married, and lived alone in a huge house on the bluff. He showed us in and indicated we'd speak in his den.

"What a great photo," I said when we entered the nicely furnished room.

Roland glanced at the photo of four men and a sailboat that had been enlarged and hung on the wall.

"That boat is my pride and joy. My one true love, if you must know."

"She's beautiful. Do you still have her?"

"I do, and if you were wondering, I go to the marina and visit her as often as I can."

"Is that you on the far left?" Jack asked after taking a step closer to the wall.

"It is," Roland answered. "The man next to me is my brother, Kurt, the man to his right is a guy Kurt worked with, Brice Jeffries, and the one to his right is a friend of ours, Clint Brown."

"It looks like you were having a good time," I observed.

"It was one of the best days of my life. The four of us had entered a local race that might not have been a big deal in the grand scheme of things, but it was a big deal to us. We took first place. It was quite an accomplishment; Brice was a last-minute replacement and had never sailed before."

"That *is* an accomplishment," I agreed. "Do Kurt and Brice live on the island?"

"No. Never did. At the time, both men lived and worked in DC. Kurt died just five years after the photo was taken and I'm not sure what ever happened to Brice."

"I'm so sorry to hear about your brother," I said.

Roland shrugged. "It was a long time ago. Now, how can I help you today?"

"As I mentioned to you on the phone," Jack began, "we're looking in to the death of Frannie Kettleman, a woman who lived on the island in 1963 and 1964. We understand you were the mayor at the time and hoped you might be able to give us some perspective regarding what led to her death."

Roland ran a hand through his thick white hair. "You mentioned on the phone that you were looking in to the Kettleman murder and that it was your opinion she hadn't been killed by the Strangler. I know your little writers' group has made a hobby of digging into old cases, and while you appear to have had some success in the past, I'm afraid you're barking up the wrong tree on this one."

"Can you elaborate?" I asked.

"I suspect it was Ned who put you up to this folly in the first place. He never was happy with the conclusion of the FBI despite the evidence staring him in the face. Ned was a good cop in his day and I know he had his doubts, but I can assure you that, as mayor of Gull Island, I was kept in the know. The FBI conducted a thorough investigation and determined, based on solid evidence, that Ms. Kettleman was simply in the wrong place at the wrong time and ended up dying at the hands of a madman. In my opinion, I don't think there's anything to find."

I frowned and glanced at Jack. He didn't seem happy either but hadn't said anything, so I asked the next question. "What about the discrepancies?"

"Discrepancies?"

"The rose, for example. It was of a different type from the one left on all the other bodies. And then there was the fact that Mrs. Kettleman was married, while the others weren't."

Roland raised a bushy white brow. "I don't know a thing about flowers, so I'm not sure I can speak to that, but I will tell you that while Mrs. Kettleman was married, as you indicated, she didn't behave like a married woman. If the Strangler was watching her, he might very well have come to the conclusion she was single. I happen to know she was within the age range and shared the same coloring as the other women. She also had the mark only the Strangler and a handful of law enforcement personnel knew about. I'm telling you, there isn't a mystery to solve. I'm sorry to disappoint you."

"I understand you and Frannie were involved in an intimate relationship at one time."

"Yes. So? I was single and she was willing. I don't think you're going to find the scandal you're looking for. I know it isn't what you want to hear, but the Strangler really was responsible for Frannie's death."

I was about to bring up the fact that Frannie had defensive wounds and may have been knocked out when stabbed, as well as the discrepancy in the width of the blade used to carve the symbol into her shoulder when Jack shook his head. I wasn't sure what was on his mind, but he didn't seem to want me to continue in that direction, so I changed the subject.

"I'm sorry we wasted your time asking about the Strangler. It's obvious you have information we don't. As long as we're here, however, do you mind if I ask about Secret Santa?"

"What do you want to know?"

"Primarily, who he is."

Roland winked. "It seems to me Secret Santa wishes to remain anonymous. But if you want my opinion of who the generous soul could be, I'd say to look for an individual who worked a lifetime serving his community and wants to continue to give back after retirement."

I raised a brow. "Are you Secret Santa?"

"Now, if I told you that, it wouldn't be a secret, would it?"

Jack indicated we should leave, so we thanked him and returned to the truck.

"What do you think?" I asked after we drove toward the tree lot,

"In terms of Frannie's death, I think Carver has made up his mind about what occurred. It isn't unusual for those in power to want to see cases closed easily and quickly. While the conclusion of the FBI lends itself to a second look in my opinion, I doubt Carver will want the case reopened even though he's no longer in office."

"Yeah, I guess I can see that. Carver certainly wouldn't be the first politician to want a case closed without indisputable evidence just to have it closed. So, what do you think about his being Secret Santa?"

Jack bit his lip. "I'm not sure. He did spend a lifetime in service to the community, and it appears he's very well off."

"But there was something so intentional about the way he told us what we wanted to know without really telling us anything."

"True. Still, I suppose it's possible he really is the man you've been looking for."

Chapter 7

We were a little early for our shift at the tree lot, but volunteer coordinator Brooke Johnson was more than happy to see us. She was in the middle of helping a customer, so she handed us each a Santa hat and told us to look around. She said she'd find us and explain what to do as soon as she completed her transaction.

I placed the red hat with its furry white brim on my head, glad I'd decided to wear a red sweater with my jeans today. It matched the hat perfectly and definitely helped to sell the Christmas idea.

"I wasn't expecting this place to be so festive," I said to Jack as we walked beneath the strings of lights overhead. The smell of gingerbread warmed and sold at the snack bar filled the air as "Rudolph the Red-Nosed Reindeer" played in the background.

"Brooke's done a good job setting a mood. If I wasn't already in the market for a tree, walking around this lot would certainly put me in the right frame of mind. If you see a tree you think is right for the resort, point it out, and I'll pay for it and store it in the truck."

I stood looking around at the sea of trees. "There are so many to choose from. I've never had a tree before, so I'm no expert when it comes to the pros and cons of the different varieties, but I do know I'd like something about eight feet tall and full. I thought I'd move the furniture away from the front window and put the tree in that little alcove. Not only will it be out of the way but we'll be able to enjoy it from the front porch and the living room."

Jack stopped to tug at the needles of a tall, thin fir. "Putting the tree in the alcove is a good idea, although you need to keep in mind it will be visible from all angles including the back, so we'll need to find one with no bare spots."

"You have high ceilings. Are you going to get a tall tree?"

"I was thinking maybe ten feet. I have room to go taller, but I don't want it to be difficult to decorate. I have a ladder, but I'd rather only have to deal with a step stool."

"I suppose you could pay a service to do the decorating. That's what my mom did every year."

"Where's the fun in that?"

"It would be more fun to decorate your own tree," I agreed. "It might not turn out as perfectly, but it would be personal. I used to ask why we couldn't get a tree to decorate together, but Mom always said no. To be honest, I don't think she would have bothered with decorations at all except for the fact that she threw a big open house every year, to which I wasn't invited."

"Not even when you got older?"

"Not even then. I'm not trying to sound pathetic or anything. My life turned out fine, so I really have no regrets."

"I guess that's something. They have coffee at the snack bar. Would you like some?"

"That sounds great. Even with the extra layers on, it's a bit on the nippy side."

By the time we had our coffee, Brooke was ready to tell us what we'd need to know during our shift. Basically, our role was to help customers find a tree they loved, ring them up, and then help them to their car. Seemed easy enough until I realized how many couples simply couldn't agree on which tree to purchase. I'd signed on to sell Christmas trees; marriage counseling was a bit out of my wheelhouse.

Once we'd been coached on the specifics, Jack and I split up, each heading to a different section of the lot. I noticed there was no Santa currently on duty, but a sign said he'd had to run to the North Pole and would be back the next day. I tried to remember whether my mother had ever taken me to see Santa when I was a child. I could remember her assistant dropping off professionally wrapped gifts to go under the tree prepped by the decorating service. I even remembered being dressed up and taken to a play at the local theater once, but I couldn't remember making a list, sitting on Santa's lap, setting out milk and cookies, or any of the other things my peers were encouraged to do.

"Excuse me, miss." A short woman with bright red hair tapped me on the shoulder.

I turned around and smiled. "How can I help you?"

"Do you have Douglas firs?"

"They're along the back fence."

"How about Silver Tips?"

I looked at the map Brooke had given us. "Just to the left of the snack bar."

"Great. See that man in the blue sweater?"

I glanced at the man she'd pointed out, who was looking at some of the flocked trees at the front of the lot. "Yes, I see him."

"He's going to come over to ask about Douglas firs. When he does, send him to the snack bar. I'll take it from there."

"I take it you want to convince him that a Silver Tip is the better tree."

"Darn right I do. Now remember: don't let him near the back of the lot."

I could see this job was going to be more challenging than I'd thought. When the man in the blue sweater asked about the Douglas firs, I told him I was new and he might want to check with the folks in the snack bar. However things ended up, I felt I'd held up my end of the bargain and set off to help a man in a dark green sweater I'd noticed wandering around near the pines at the far edge of the lot.

"Can I help you?" I asked the man, whose back was to me. When he turned around, I almost fainted on the spot. "Dru?" After a brief hesitation, I threw myself into his arms. "What are you doing here?"

"I could say I was here to buy a tree, but you'd see right through that, so I guess I'll be honest and say I'm here to see you."

I took a step back and looked at the man I'd worked with for five years, dating him for two of them, before he'd taken a job in Los Angeles and I hadn't followed him. "You're here to see me? Why?"

"Again, I could say because I missed you, which I have, but the truth of the matter is, Margo sent me."

"Margo?" I looked around to make sure no one was listening before I continued. "You flew all the way to South Carolina from Los Angeles to try to talk me into taking a job in New York?"

"Actually, I flew from New York to South Carolina. I'm working for Margo at the magazine now. When you come on board it'll be the three of us together again, just the way it used to be."

I stared in stunned silence at the handsome, dark-haired man I once assumed I'd have a life with. Dru was back in New York? There was a time when that would have thrilled me, but that was in the past; now I was just confused. "You're working for Margo?" I parroted, even though that was exactly what Dru had just said.

He nodded, "I was already getting a little antsy in LA, so when Margo called with her offer, I couldn't refuse. I jumped at the chance to come back to the East Coast." Dru paused and looked me in the eye. "I jumped at the chance to come back to you."

Dru pulled me into his arms and kissed me hard on the mouth. I was so shocked, I just stood there. After I finally had the presence of mind to take a step back, I looked around only to see Jack watching us from a distance.

"Come to dinner with me," Dru said. "It'll give us a chance to catch up and talk about the magazine."

"I can't go to dinner. I'm working."

"You work at a tree lot?"

"I volunteer at a tree lot. How did you find me here anyway?"

"Vikki. You changed your cell number and I couldn't get hold of Margo, but Vikki had the same number she's always had, so I called her when I got to the island and she told me I could find you here."

I was kind of surprised Vikki had told him where I was. Of course, she was one of the few people on earth who knew how much Dru's leaving had destroyed me, and how I'd hoped he would return to my part of the world one day. Like the job offer from Margo, if he'd shown up even a few months ago, I would have jumped at the offer for dinner.

"I'm happy to see you. I really am. And I do want to have a chance to get caught up. But not only do I have to finish my shift here, I have plans this evening. How about breakfast?"

"Okay, if I must wait that long. Nine o'clock?"

"Nine will work. There's a café on the pier named Gertie's. I'll meet you there."

"It sounds like you're saying good-bye for now."

I nodded. "I really do need to get back to work. We can talk tomorrow."

Dru didn't look happy, but he didn't argue. He quickly kissed me on the lips and I watched him walk toward his rental car.

"Do I want to ask?" Jack said when he came over to where I was still standing after Dru left.

"That was a man I used to work with."

"Worked with?"

"And dated," I added reluctantly. "I haven't seen him since he moved to LA five years ago. I was shocked when I went over to a man to help him and it turned out to be him."

"Is he visiting someone on the island?"

I looked Jack in the eye. "He's here to see me. I have something to talk to you about, but not here. After our shift."

Jack frowned. "Okay. I'm curious, but I guess I can wait."

"We'll grab some dinner and I'll tell you everything. I promise."

******

By the time our shift was over, the diner down the street was all but empty, so we decided to eat there. I chose the prime rib sandwich, Jack the meatloaf special. Once our orders had been placed and our drinks delivered, I began the tale I wished I had more time to prepare for. Still, I owed Jack an explanation, and I'd been putting off telling him about the job offer long enough.

"I first met Dru when I was just starting out. He and I and a woman named Margo Bronson all worked for this underground newspaper no one had really heard of at that point. We were young and idealistic, and the most important thing to us was digging for the truth and exposing it to the world." I smiled. "It really was one of the best times in my life."

"The energy and idealism of youth is hard to beat," Jack agreed.

"Anyway, the three of us were something of a team, bonding the way good friends with a common goal often do. Not only did we work together but we pooled our income and rented a three-bedroom apartment in a decent part of the city. We were like a family, and after growing up feeling as if I'd never really had a family, it meant a lot to me."

I could see Jack was listening intently, but he didn't stop me.

"After a few years, Dru got a job working for a major television station. It was a great job with a huge salary, but his office was across town, so Dru moved to his own place. Margo, who was the go-getter of the three of us, got a job with a news magazine that was just starting up, and I moved to the newspaper I was eventually fired from. Although we no longer worked or lived together, we were still really close and got together for dinner and drinks two or three times a week."

I took a breath and blew it out slowly before I continued. "Then, seven years ago, Dru and I started dating. We'd known each other for a long time by then, and things progressed quickly. Eventually, we found an apartment halfway between his job and mine, and I thought we were going to make a go of it. Then, five years ago, just four months after we signed the lease on that apartment, Dru was offered a wonderful job at another television station in LA. It was a huge promotion, much too good to pass up. So, he took it. He wanted me to go with him, but I decided my own career was in New York and too important to me, so I stayed there."

Jack still hadn't said anything, but I couldn't help but notice the frown on his face. I wanted to stop there, but I knew I had to tell him everything.

"Shortly after Dru left, Margo took a big job at another magazine. We were still close, but we were both busy with our careers and, to be honest, without Dru prodding us to take the time we needed to ensure our continued friendship, we sort of faded away. At least until I was fired. Margo virtually put her own job aside to make sure I was going to be okay. She was a huge support to me when I was going through my crisis, and when I moved to Gull Island, she promised to keep her eye open and call me if something opened up. She called me yesterday. She was recently made managing director for a large news magazine and offered me a job."

"In New York?"

"In New York," I confirmed.

"And…? Did you take it?"

"Not yet. I told her I needed to think about it and she gave me until Monday. I planned to tell you, but I wanted to get things straight in my head first. No one knows about the offer except Vikki and, apparently, Dru. Margo sent him here to try to sweeten the pot."

"Dru flew in from LA to convince you to take a job in New York?"

I shook my head. "He moved back to New York to work for Margo. Years ago, when we were working at that little underground newspaper, we used to talk about all of us working together for a major publication one day."

"So, you *are* going to move?" I noticed the slight catch in his voice.

"I don't know," I said honestly. "Margo's offer is something I've always dreamed of. Working with them again was something I wanted more than anything at one point in my life. Six months ago, I would have jumped at the chance. But now…now I have a new life I've come to love to consider."

Jack took a deep breath and let it out slowly. "Thank you for telling me. You know I want you to stay, but I won't put any undue pressure on you while you make up your mind. It sounds like you have a lot to consider."

"I do. And thank you. I've spent a lot of time thinking about this over the past twenty-four hours, but right now I just want to have dinner with you, then decorate the tree at the resort with the others."

Jack put his hand over mine and gave it a squeeze. He tried to smile, but I saw the worry in his eyes.

Chapter 8

Thursday, December 14

I woke up early the next morning and decided to take a walk before getting ready to meet Dru. Even though things had started off rough at dinner the night before, Jack and I had ended up having a wonderful time with the writers decorating the tree, eating the goodies Clara had baked, and watching *It's a Wonderful Life* as it played in the background. I was sorry when Jack left, but I had breakfast with Dru and thinking to do in the meantime.

Of all the times for Margo's offer to come through and Dru to show up, this was probably the worst. If both had occurred earlier—even a couple of months earlier—I'd already be on my way to New York, and if they'd happened a bit further into the future, I'd probably have a better idea of how things were going to work out on Gull Island and with Jack. But as things stood now, there was just a lot of promise mixed with a generous dollop of uncertainty.

I paused to watch the waves roll onto the shore. When I'd lived in New York, I'd given little thought to living surrounded by concrete and skyscrapers. It had never occurred to me to long for quiet moments, open space, and the beauty of nature, but after living on Gull Island for almost six months, I knew without a shadow of a doubt that if I returned to my urban lifestyle, I would miss the simplicity of a sun rising from the horizon beyond the sea, the gulls flying overhead, and the gentle rhythm of waves rolling onto the shore.

I thought about Jack and his gentle and funny ways. If I left now, I'd always wonder what we could have had and who we might have become. I thought about George and Clara and the others who lived at the retreat and knew I would miss every one of them. I was fairly certain Garrett would adapt and do fine without me, but I'd just found him, and there was a part of me that really wanted to give us the chance we needed to become the family I'd always longed for.

And then, on the other side of the coin, there were Margo, Dru, and New York. I remembered those early days, when the three of us had worked together. We'd vowed to take on the world, and in many ways, we had. We'd not only worked hard but played hard too. We really had been living the dream, or at least the beginning of it. I'd known Vikki most of my life and she'd always been and always would be my best friend, but during those years in New York, when we were both busy building our careers, we'd lived very different lives, so Dru and Margo had become my whole world. There was no denying how much they'd meant to me. Could I turn down the chance to work with them again? Revisit a part of my life that had meant so much to me?

Margo would be hurt if I turned her down. I suspected she already was. In her mind, I was sure she'd imagined her offer would be greeted with complete enthusiasm. And I really did wish that could had been my response. Of all the people in my professional life, she had done the most for me.

I turned and began walking back to the house. I had my breakfast with Dru and then two meetings Jack had set up with people who had known Frannie Kettleman. The first, which was set for eleven o'clock, was with Wes Gardner. Like the others we'd already spoken to, he was retired, but he once owned a used bookstore and remembered Frannie coming in to check out the new stock each week. The second, at two o'clock, was with Clint Brown, the local Realtor Edna had told us she'd seen Frannie having dinner with. Sherry had thought Frannie had been looking to buy property on the island. If that was the case, Clint might be able to give us some insight regarding her frame of mind.

"I thought I might find you out here," Vikki greeted me as I neared the house.

"I wasn't expecting to find you up this early."

"I'm usually not, but your situation with Dru and Margo has been weighing on my mind. I saw you walk by on your way out and wanted to get an update. I wanted to talk to you last night, but we were never alone."

"There isn't a lot to tell. Dru is working for Margo now and living back in New York. He's here to help talk me into taking Margo's offer. We haven't had much of a chance to talk yet. I'm meeting him for breakfast."

"Does Jack know about him?"

I nodded. "He saw us talking at the tree lot and asked about him. I told him everything afterward. Well, almost everything. I may have left out the part that, until now, I considered Dru the one real love of my life: the one who got away."

"Until now?" Vikki took my hand in hers and started walking back to the house.

"Now, I have Jack. I don't know if what we might have will ever come close to what I had with Dru, but I care about our relationship enough to want to see where it takes us. Margo's offer is very tempting, but there's a lot I'd be giving up if I leave the island. I don't know how I'm going to decide."

Vikki put her arm around my shoulders and pulled me close. "I think when it comes down to it, you'll know what you want. In fact, I bet you already do."

I wished I could be as certain as Vikki that I knew what I wanted. When I thought of Jack, the resort, my friends, and the life I'd so recently built, I knew I wanted all of it. But then I thought of Margo, Dru, New York, and the chance to write news for a major platform, and I knew I wanted that as well. I knew the two lives couldn't mesh, so I'd have to choose one or the other, but I had no idea which life I wanted more.

I was just about to get undressed to take a shower when my phone rang. "Hello?"

"This is Colin Walton. I have a message that you wanted me to call you. Is there a problem with Garrett?"

"No, Garrett's fine. Garrett's great, in fact, and I'm very grateful for everything you and your staff have done for him. I wanted to speak to you about Secret Santa. I want to interview him for an article I'm writing, and someone suggested you and he might be one and the same."

Colin chuckled. "I'm afraid I'm not Secret Santa. I have my niche in the community and he has his."

"I sort of figured that out already, but I'd already left the message for you before I really thought it through. But do you know who Secret Santa is?"

"I don't, and if I did, I wouldn't say. It seems to me Secret Santa has a reason to want to keep his identity to himself. Perhaps you should respect that."

"Don't you think he should get the recognition he deserves?"

"Recognition can be shallow. I've found it isn't all it's cracked up to be. What really fills your soul is the knowledge you made a significant difference in the life of others. To be honest, receiving accolades for your contribution sort of cheapens it. I find knowing you acted selflessly is a much sweeter reward."

"I guess you have a point. Thank you for speaking to me. And I promise, even if I do figure out who Secret Santa is, I won't out him if he doesn't want to be."

******

Dru was waiting for me when I arrived at Gertie's. I noticed she still wasn't working the counter, so I could only imagine her date in Charleston was going even better than she'd imagined. I was really happy for her. I wasn't privy to her entire romantic history, but it seemed to me she'd been alone much of her life, and as far as I could tell, Quinten Davenport was perfect for her.

I waved to Dru as I started across the café toward him. He looked good this morning, in a pair of khakis topped with a light blue polo shirt and a royal blue V-neck sweater.

"Sorry I'm late," I said as I slid into the booth across from the man I'd once thought I might marry.

"You aren't late; I was early." Dru waved at the waitress, who brought me a cup of coffee. "How was your evening?"

"Really fun. The writers who live at the resort and I decorated our Christmas tree. It came out beautifully. You'll have to stop by to see it before you leave."

"You know I'm not here to look at Christmas trees."

I took a sip of my coffee. "I know. I guess I was just trying to prolong the inevitable conversation we're about to have."

"Sounds dire."

I shrugged. "I'm just stressed about how this will go. I know how important it is to Margo that I take the job. I love you both and don't want to let either of you down."

"So don't let us down. Take the job. You have to admit it's even better than the jobs we used to dream of."

I looked down at my hands. "It's a fantastic job and the thought of working with you and Margo again is very tempting, but I've made a life here. A life I love."

"You used to love your life in New York. Maybe you will again."

"Maybe. I've been remembering the fun we had and the dreams we shared. Those first years before any of us were a blip on the radar were some of the best of my life. But that's the past. Things have changed. I've changed."

Dru's voice softened. "It sounds like you've made up your mind."

I shook my head. "No, I haven't. At least not about the job."

Dru frowned. "So, that means you've made up your mind about us."

I didn't answer immediately. Finally, I said, "There isn't an us. Not anymore. I really did love you when we were dating, and maybe I should have followed you to LA, but I didn't, and that choice, I think, decided our future."

"It doesn't have to."

"Actually, I think it sort of does. It's been five years. As I said before, things have changed and so have we. When you first left I wasn't sure I could make it through the pain, but now it feels like a distant memory."

Dru took my hand in his. "I really did miss you." He rested our joined hands on the table between us. "I must have second-guessed my leaving New York a hundred times during that first year. Every time I thought of your smile or imagined your laugh, I could feel my heart being ripped from my chest."

"It was the same for me. I picked up the phone dozens of times, intending to call you to say I'd changed my mind and would be on the next flight west. But I never did call you and you never called me. We made our choice and now, with perspective, I think it was the right one for both of us."

Dru didn't answer right away, but I saw the sadness in his eyes. When he spoke, he asked, "Is there someone else?"

"Yes. His name is Jack and we've been dating for a few months. Our relationship is new and it isn't based on a history, the way ours was, but I really want to have the opportunity to see where it takes us. The idea of leaving Jack is one of the reasons I'm not sure about the job, but it isn't the only reason. I have something here on the island I haven't had for a long time: a family. The writers who live and work at the resort are more than just friends; they're people whose lives I've become a part of. The offer Margo made me is better than anything I've ever hoped for or imagined, but when I think of leaving the life I've built here, I die a little inside."

"You may not get an offer like this again."

"I know. And there's a part of me—a big part— that misses the day-to-day world of journalism. While I have a wonderful social life on the island, I'll admit I've been floundering professionally. I've done some freelance work, but the opportunity to work with you and Margo, to ride the magazine into the number-one spot, really does seem too good to pass up."

Our conversation paused when the waitress brought our food. I was just as glad; it gave me a minute to get my emotions under control.

"I'm sorry I can't be more certain one way or the other," I said at last.

"I understand. It sounds like you have a big decision ahead of you."

"I do. And while I've loved seeing you again, it's a decision I need to make on my own."

Dru began buttering his toast. "I agree. I've booked a flight for tomorrow morning. In the meantime, I'd love it if you could show me the island. I'd hate for us not to spend the time we have together."

"You make it sound like one of us is dying."

Dru laughed. "I guess that was a bit melodramatic. How about it? Can you spend the day with me?"

I grimaced. "I'm sorry. I'd love to, but I have meetings this afternoon."

"Okay, then how about dinner? I'll pick you up and you can show me this resort you're so fond of."

"Okay," I said. "But an early dinner. Say six?"

"Six is fine."

I gave Dru directions to the resort, then set off for the paper to meet Jack. I felt bad about what I was putting him through. If an old girlfriend of his came to town and was monopolizing his time, I think I'd find the experience pretty darn miserable, and the very last thing I wanted to do was to make Jack unhappy.

Chapter 9

Wes Gardner lived in a small house just a block off the main road that ran through town. He was the oldest of all the witnesses we'd interviewed so far at eighty-eight, but his mind was sharp and he'd seemed happy to have the company when Jack called to ask if he'd be willing to take some time out of his day to speak to us. I supposed by the time you were eighty-eight, you didn't have a lot of company or a lot of activity to fill your days.

"Thank you for meeting with us," Jack said as he put a hand on the small of my back and ushered me inside when Wes stood aside and indicated we should enter.

"I was happy to have the opportunity to chat with you. Frannie was such a sweet thing. A pretty girl, and so full of life. It was a damn shame what happened to her."

Wes led us down a narrow hallway to an enclosed porch where we all took seats on the wicker couches.

"How can I help you exactly?" he asked.

"When we spoke on the phone you mentioned she would sit with you for a spell when she came by the bookstore," Jack said. "Do you mind sharing what you talked about?"

Wes tilted his head of white hair to one side. "Books mostly. Frannie was a voracious reader. She checked out a lot of things from the library, but that selection was relatively limited, and she ran out of romance and mystery novels that interested her. She began coming into the bookstore to look at my inventory, which, unlike the library's, changed all the time. She didn't have much money, so we worked out a deal where she could borrow books. She'd take three of four books, read them, and bring them back to exchange them for three or four different ones."

"That was very nice of you," I said.

Wes shrugged. "Frannie was a sweet girl. I think she was lonely, and reading was her escape. She was very appreciative of my offer and I was happy to help her out. Anyway, when she came in to exchange books, if I'd read a book she'd recently finished, we would discuss it. She'd tell me what she liked and didn't like, and I'd do the same. If she read a book I hadn't, she'd tell me about it and then offer an opinion as to whether she thought I'd like it or not. Occasionally, our conversations would lead to other subjects."

"Can you expand on that?" Jack asked.

"Once, Frannie read a book set in Scotland. I'd visited there as a young man, so we spoke quite a bit about the scenery and customs. She'd ask questions to get a clear image in her mind and I'd do my best to answer them. We also discussed sailing and hiking, two things I'd done a lot of but she hadn't gotten around to. And she was fascinated by local history, so we chatted about that. We talked about dozens of things."

"Did she ever talk to you about her marriage?" Jack asked.

"Not really. I knew her young man had been drafted and was in Vietnam. Although she never said so, I got the idea she was just as glad he was away. She did say something once that led me to believe she'd only married the man because her father made her."

It seemed odd to think of a forced marriage in the sixties, but fathers often did have a huge influence over the decisions their daughters made even then.

"Did Frannie ever talk to you about her friendships on the island, male and female?" Jack asked.

"We didn't discuss our personal lives much at all. I heard rumors she had men on the side, but she never mentioned them to me, and it wasn't my business, so I never asked."

"Did she ever mention someone named Paul?" I wondered.

A thoughtful expression came across Wes's face. "That name did come up. She'd read a book in which there was a character named Nick, who was in love with Rita, someone he could never have. Of course, that didn't stop Nick from courting Rita. He'd send her letters and buy her little trinkets. Frannie made a comment about the character reminding her of someone named Paul. She said he was in love with her and she'd strung him along, though the love was very one-sided. I said something about letting him know how she really felt and she said Paul provided her a level of protection that made dealing with his endless letters worth the effort."

This revelation that Frannie hadn't felt about Paul the way he did about her made me sad. The letters had seemed so romantic when we'd first found them.

"A level of protection?" Jack murmured.

"She didn't elaborate and I didn't ask. As I indicted before, we tended to keep our personal lives out of our conversations."

I noticed the expression on Wes's face had changed since we'd begun to chat. His smile had faded and his eyes had narrowed, making him seem more contemplative.

"If Frannie wasn't killed by the Strangler, as most people believe, can you guess who might have done it?" I asked.

Wes tilted his head. "I really can't. Frannie was a beautiful girl. She had the sort of presence that caused men and women alike to stop and turn their heads when she walked down the street. In a way, it isn't surprising she ended up a victim. She was like a light that drew in the moths, but once she had them, she seemed to have little use for them. Not that I know that for a fact. Based on her comments about the characters in the books she read, I'd little doubt she used and then discarded people along the way."

"Do you remember the last time you saw her?" Jack asked.

"It must have been a couple of weeks, maybe three, before her death. She came in looking for books on childbirth. She told me a friend was pregnant and she wanted to help her find out what to expect. She also said her husband was coming home and he didn't like her to read so much, so she wasn't sure whether she'd be in again. As it turned out, that was the last time I ever saw her."

"Did she say why her husband didn't like her to read?" I asked, scandalized by the very idea that any man would have a problem with his wife reading.

"She didn't say, but I got the feeling he was very rigid."

Jack and I thanked Wes and then headed out to his truck. We both took a few notes, then headed to Clint Brown's home. I felt we were learning a lot about Frannie's personality as well as her actions during her final days, but I wasn't sure we were any closer to nailing the identity of the person who'd killed her.

"Oh darn; I forgot to ask him about Secret Santa," I said after we'd pulled away from Wes's house.

"It would have been a tough segue between the two subjects."

"Yeah, you're right. The times I've brought it up have been awkward. One minute we're discussing the brutal murder of a young woman and the next I'm asking about the personification of a mythical character living right here on the island. Besides. I'm thinking of dropping the whole thing anyway."

"I don't disagree that dropping it would be best, but you seemed so anxious to figure out who Secret Santa is. What changed your mind?"

"A lot of people have made the point that Secret Santa's identity is a secret for a reason. If I had to guess, I'd say Evan Paddington is our guy. Roland Carver seemed to indicate he was, but the history behind the legend fits Evan better. I suppose if I ever have an opportunity to speak to Evan about his role in the community I might do it just to assuage my curiosity, but as far as the article goes, I think the truth behind Secret Santa will remain a secret, at least for the time being."

"I'm glad to hear that. I thought it was sort of sad to unmask the man. It would be like unmasking Batman."

"Oh, I'd unmask Batman in a minute."

Jack grinned. "Do you want to have dinner at my house tonight? We still need to decorate my tree, and I bought a new wine you might like."

I groaned. "I really, really do want to help you with your tree, but I promised Dru I'd have dinner with him tonight."

Jack's smile faded. "I understand. We can do it another time."

"I don't think you do understand. I would much rather spend the evening with you, but Dru is leaving in the morning and he asked if we could spend the day together to catch up on old times, but I told him I had meetings this afternoon. He suggested dinner and I didn't feel I could turn him down. We've been friends a long time."

"It really is okay." Jack tried for another smile. "We can do the tree another time."

"You know," I said, placing my hand on his leg, "we're meeting early for dinner and I promised to show him the resort, but we shouldn't be too late. I could come over after."

Jack's smile was authentic this time. "I'd like that."

"And I'll bring a bag with a few things in it. Just in case."

Jack's grin got bigger. "Just in case."

******

Clint lived in a huge home overlooking the ocean. He'd been in real estate for a long time and, apparently, he'd found quite the perfect home for himself. Unlike the other people we'd spoken to, who were all currently single, Clint was currently married to a beautiful woman in her early forties, although he was in his midseventies. His wife wasn't home today, however, which allowed us to speak freely without danger of being overheard.

"As you know from our conversation on the phone, we're looking in to Frannie Kettleman's death fifty-three years ago. One of the people we spoke to mentioned you'd been seen having dinner with her, so we wanted to ask about her interest in real estate on the island," Jack began.

Clint laughed out loud. A deep, thundering laugh that couldn't help but get my attention.

"Is that funny?"

"I just figured if you wanted to talk to me about Frannie's death, you were looking for information regarding our dalliance, not her interest in real estate."

"Your dalliance?" I asked.

Clint chuckled again. "I guess you really didn't know. Maybe I shouldn't have let the cat out of the bag."

"Maybe you shouldn't, but because you have, would you care to elaborate?" I asked.

"Frannie was a pretty girl who knew how to use her assets to get what she wanted. She came into my life when my first wife was pregnant with our first child. Frannie made it clear she was only interested in a relationship in the physical sense, and I gave in to her seduction and cheated on my wife. My wife has since passed and my children hate me for marrying a woman younger than my eldest, but I still wouldn't want this paraded around town, if you don't mind keeping it to yourself."

"And your dalliance—was it just the one time?" I asked.

"Not that it's any of your business, but yes, it was just the one time."

"I only asked because we've been told Frannie was pregnant when she died."

"Not surprising, but I wasn't the father. We were together almost a year before she was murdered."

"You said Frannie used her 'assets' to get what she wanted," Jack said. "Did she want something from you?"

"Yes, she did. She wanted money. A lot of it. After we slept together, she told me she was hard up for cash, and while she never came out and said she'd tell my wife what we'd done if I didn't give her the money, she implied it."

"How much did you give her?" I wondered.

"Ten grand. At the time it stung quite a bit, but looking back, it was worth it. That girl knew her way around the bedroom, if you know what I mean. Talk about enthusiasm."

Suddenly, the bad taste in my mouth became much sourer. I was tempted to ask for a glass of water, but I just wanted to finish the interview and get out of Brown's house. "Did Frannie ever ask you for additional money?"

"No. And if you're thinking blackmail could have been a motive for her murder, I'd say you might be on to something. But I didn't kill her. I was out of the country for the ten days prior to and two weeks after Frannie's death. You can check with the FBI. I provided documentation to them when they interviewed me."

"Do you remember the name of the person who interviewed you?" I asked.

"No. It was a long time ago. Are you thinking you might need to check out the validity of what I've told you?"

"It did enter my mind."

"Save your energy. I had no reason to kill Frannie. Despite her bilking me out of ten grand, I really liked her. She had a sunny disposition and was pleasant to be around. I don't know who killed her, but if I was the one investigating the case, I'd take a serious look at the men in her life at the time of her death. What Frannie and I had was brief, which was exactly what we were both looking for, but I wouldn't be surprised at all to hear there were other men in her life who wanted something more than she was able to give."

"You think there may have been men who fell in love with her?"

"That's exactly what I'm saying. Frannie could entice men to fall in love with her, but she wasn't capable of giving love in return. The girl was damaged goods, if you ask me."

I wanted to make a comment about his being damaged goods as well but didn't. I supposed in a crude way Cliff had provided us with another piece of the puzzle, as well as another motive for Frannie's murder. I'd thought by this point we'd have a clear picture of what had been going on in her life that could have led to her death, but it seemed the more people we spoke to, the cloudier things became.

Chapter 10

Friday, December 15

I woke with a smile on my face. Jack's arms were wrapped around me so tightly, I felt as if he might never let me go, which was okay with me. I'd had a nice dinner with Dru the evening before. We'd had a lot of catching up to do, and by the end of the evening, I'd forgotten all about the huge decision I had to make and was laughing at his jokes, the way I always did. It was fun showing him around the brightly decorated island, but by the end of the evening, I couldn't wait to say good-bye and join Jack, who I knew was waiting for me. Dru had been an important part of my life, and there was a part of me that would always love him, but for the first time since he'd left New York, I was certain I was no longer *in* love with him.

"Good morning, beautiful," Jack said after kissing me on the neck.

I turned onto my side and looked him in the eye. "When you first suggested I stay over here occasionally, I wasn't sure about it, but I have to admit I could get used to this."

Jack smiled. "You're welcome to stay as often as you like. Are you hungry?"

"Not for food."

******

"You're late," Vikki said. I was supposed to meet her for a late breakfast, but one thing had led to another this morning and I was almost twenty minutes late.

"I know." I couldn't help the grin I was sure stretched from ear to ear on my face.

"Oh God, you didn't sleep with Dru?"

"What? No! Of course not. If you must know, I stayed over with Jack."

Vikki frowned. "Didn't I see you leave the resort last night with Dru?"

"You did. We went to dinner and I showed him around town, but then I asked him to bring me home. I grabbed my car and headed over to Jack's. Didn't you notice my car was gone?"

"I guess I wasn't paying that much attention. So, what's going on with Dru? And Margo? And Jack, for that matter. I'm your best friend, but somehow I feel totally out of the loop."

"You aren't out of the loop," I assured her as I waved to the server, indicating I'd like a cup of coffee. "In fact, other than Jack, you know more than anyone else. Still, I know how you feel when your best friend is going through a personal crisis and you want to help, so I'll try to fill you in."

Vikki sat back in the booth. "You're going through a crisis?"

"A crisis of indecision. But I'll loop back to that. As for Jack, I told him about Dru. All of it. I don't think he was happy he was in town, but he seems to be dealing just fine with it. I've spent the night at his place three times in the past week, and we discussed my bringing over a few things to keep at his place."

"Are you moving in with him?"

"No, not moving in. Just staying there occasionally. And he's going to stay at the resort sometimes as well."

"So you're staying on Gull Island?"

I let out a breath. "I'm still not sure. I know I'm no longer in love with Dru, and things are going so well with Jack that I do want to see that through. Still, there's a part of my decision that has nothing to do with either of them. The job Margo is offering is a once-in-a-lifetime opportunity. I'd be in a position to have my voice heard. To make a difference. And that really appeals to me. I love the personal life I have here. I love the family at the retreat, and of course I love having Jack in my life, but professionally, I feel sort of stagnant. When I came to the island I was going to take a few months, help Garrett until he could return to the resort, write the book I've been talking about for half my life, and then go back to what I'd left behind once things cooled down. I've been here since June, and while I've helped Garrett as I intended, I haven't done a thing to move my career forward."

"You've written some freelance pieces."

"I have, but Margo is offering me a career and a lifestyle. The thing is, I'm not sure if it's a lifestyle I still want."

"I guess you do have some more thinking to do."

"I do, but she's only given me until Monday to decide, so I need to think fast. I feel like it should be an easy decision, but it isn't. If I turn this job down, I'll most likely never have another opportunity like it. But if I leave…"

Vikki put her hand over mine. "Whatever you decide, I'll always be here for you."

"I know. And that means a lot to me. And Garrett will still be my brother, and I'm sure if I leave the island, he'll welcome me back for visits. But it won't be the same, and I won't have Jack." I wiped a tear from my cheek. "What am I going to do?"

"I don't know, sweetie. It seems whichever choice you make you'll have to give something up. Maybe instead of looking at which option will provide the biggest gain, you should ask yourself what you can't bear to lose."

"That helps. Thanks."

"So, are you and Jack sleuthing again today?"

I shook my head. "Actually, no. It's a print day at the paper, so he's busy all day, although he'll be at the Mastermind meeting tonight. I thought I might finish the decorating out at the resort. And I need to run by the market to pick up the ingredients for dinner."

Vikki finished her coffee. "I'm free today, so I'll help you. Instead of eating now, let's run to the market, take the groceries back to the resort, and then make an inventory of what we still need in terms of decorations. Then we can come back into town to get what we need. I'll even buy you lunch at that new café on Gull Avenue."

"Sounds perfect."

******

The new café seemed to me to be on the upscale side for casual Gull Island, but the food looked delicious and the black furniture with the bright red tablecloths looked nice with the deep red carpet. Vikki ordered an ahi salad and I settled on an abalone steak on a flaky croissant.

"I may have to save room for dessert," I said as I folded a black napkin onto my lap. "Whatever the couple at that table in the corner is having looked delicious."

"I've heard the tarts are fabulous, and you know I always love a good cobbler." Vikki pushed the vase with a single red rose off to the side to make way for the pad of paper she'd brought with her. "I made a list of everything we need to finish the decorating at the resort, but I don't think we'll be able to find the fabric I've been envisioning for the tree skirt."

"Don't most people just use a sheet?"

Vikki looked scandalized. "A sheet?"

"I have a red one. It'll look nice, and it can go back to being a sheet when it's done being a tree skirt."

Vikki shrugged. "Okay. Sounds okay by me. I'm not going to be there on Christmas anyway."

I took a sip of my water before responding. "I think it's wonderful you're going to spend Christmas with Rick. And that you're going to meet his family."

"Yeah, I guess." Vikki had begun nervously folding and unfolding the corner of her napkin. "I'm nervous about the family part."

"Why would you be nervous? You meet new people all the time."

Vikki tucked a lock of her long hair behind her ear. "I know, but this is different. I really like Rick and I want his family to like me."

"They'll love you." I could tell by the look on Vikki's face that she was less than confident. I decided to change the subject to do away with this element of stress over lunch. "I got a card from my mom the other day."

Vikki raised a brow. "A card? Wow, that's new."

"I know. I was shocked. In all my thirty-eight years, she's never sent me so much as a birthday card, and certainly not a Christmas card. And there's more. There was a gift certificate inside."

"Wow. She got you a gift?"

"If a gift card for a day spa in LA can be considered a gift, yes."

"Why on earth would she get you a gift card for a spa in LA when you live in South Carolina?"

I laughed. "I think she must have had it on hand. It expires in two weeks."

Vikki rolled her eyes. "Now that sounds like the woman I know. Still, a card is more than you've ever received from her before. I suppose you should feel good about the fact that she was thinking of you."

"I do. I even invited her to come out here at some point to visit, although I doubt she will. She thinks the only city worth visiting on this side of the country is New York. I imagine if I want to see her I'll have to go to her at some point."

"Would that be so bad? LA is lovely in the spring."

"It is lovely, and I'm sure I'll visit, but it seems every time I see her, Mom is so busy we hardly speak and I end up feeling angry and resentful that I went to all the trouble to make the trip and she couldn't be bothered to spend more than two minutes with me."

Vikki didn't respond, but I knew she understood.

"Say, isn't that the girl who used to work for Gertie?" Vikki asked. "The one from the case we worked on last fall."

"Carrie," I supplied as I waved to the girl, who smiled and headed in our direction. Had it only been two months since we'd worked our first case as the Mastermind group?

"Jill. How are you?" Carrie greeted me.

"I'm well. This is my friend Vikki."

"It's nice to meet you. I recognize you from Gertie's."

"It's nice to meet you as well," Vikki replied.

"Have you left the island?" I asked. "I haven't seen you there lately."

"Yes. After everything that happened back in October, I decided it was time to move on. I got a job in Charleston, but I have today off, so I'm on the island to have lunch with a friend who should be here any moment."

"I'm glad things worked out for you."

"My job is fun and I get to meet a lot of people. Even better, there aren't any bad memories wrapped up with the people or the atmosphere. I haven't been able to so much as look at a boat since all those suppressed memories came flooding back."

"I don't blame you. It was a pretty bad situation."

Carrie turned and looked toward the door. "Oh, my friend's here. I should go. Have a nice lunch. It was great seeing you again."

"Same here, and good luck with the new job."

I watched Carrie walk across the room. Seeing her here today stirred up a niggling memory, something that felt as if it could be important, but I couldn't quite pull it up.

"Something wrong?" Vikki asked after a minute. "You're scowling."

"No, nothing's wrong I just got a feeling there was something important I needed to remember."

"I hate when that happens. I'm sure it'll come to you."

"Yeah. I'm sure it will."

We were quiet as our food was delivered. It looked delicious. I hadn't had abalone for years, but I remembered that, if prepared well, it was one of the best-tasting things to come from the sea.

Vikki and I ate in silence for several minutes before she spoke. "By the way, I need you to help me remember to talk to Alex about a boat Rick's friend is selling. Alex mentioned to Rick a while back that he was thinking about buying a boat if he could get a good deal on one."

"The boat. That's it."

"Huh?" Vikki looked confused.

"Seeing Carrie, who was involved in an investigation regarding a boat, reminded me that I wanted to think more about a photo of a boat I saw in Roland Carver's home."

Vikki frowned. "Maybe you should back up a bit; this isn't making sense to me."

"When Jack and I visited the home of ex-Mayor Roland Carver, I saw a large photo on the wall of four men standing in front of a boat. They'd just won a local sailing race and took the photo to memorialize the event. What I noticed but didn't have time to explore was that Roland and his brother were both tall and thin with thick blond hair. They looked very much like the man in the photo with Frannie who I initially thought could be my father. I see no reason why Roland's brother would be embracing Frannie, but Roland admitted to having a fling with her, so he could very well be the man in the photo. I meant to take another look at that photo, but I forgot all about it."

"Wait; Frannie had an affair with the mayor?"

"So it would seem. As far as I can tell, Frannie was involved with several men while she lived on the island. In fact, two men have admitted as much."

"I have to say, the story of long-distance romance I initially envisioned has taken a decidedly unromantic turn."

"Yeah. It seems Frannie was a beautiful woman with the sort of energy people were drawn to, but it doesn't seem as if she took love, romance, and marriage seriously. Anyway, remind me to look at the photo again when we get home. I find I much prefer the thought that it was Roland embracing Frannie than my father."

After we finished our meal, we headed to the store that sold decorations. Things were beginning to become somewhat picked over, but we didn't need a lot, and if we couldn't find everything on the list I was sure Vikki, who was supercreative, would find a way to improvise.

"Jill," a woman said from behind me.

I turned around. "Edna. How are you?"

"Fine. I just needed to pick up a few things before the weekend."

"This is my friend Vikki. Vikki, this is Edna Turner. She used to be the town librarian."

"Vikki? Are you Victoria Vance, the romance author?" Edna asked.

"I am. I'm happy to meet you, Edna."

Edna put a hand to her chest. "Oh my. I'm so happy to meet you. I love your books."

"Thank you." Vikki smiled. "I appreciate that."

"I wish I knew I was going to run into you. I would have brought a book for you to sign."

"I have a few in my car. I'll run out and get one for you."

"That would be wonderful."

Edna looked at me while Vikki was gone. "I can't believe you know Victoria Vance. You know, they're making a movie out of one of her books."

"Yes, I know. Vikki and I have been friends for most of our lives. I'm glad you had the opportunity to meet her."

"I'm thrilled. And I'm glad I ran into you. I remembered something else after you left and even considered calling you."

"Oh? What was it?"

"Frannie came into the library a couple of months before she was murdered. She had a black eye and scratches on her face. I asked her what had happened and she said she'd been hiking and had fallen down a hill. I didn't argue with her, but that eye didn't look at all like the sort of thing that happens from a slip and fall."

"You think someone hit her?"

"I'm sure of it. Frannie wasn't the skittish sort. She was quite outgoing, but when I saw her after that, she displayed a tendency to flinch whenever she heard a loud noise. I tried to talk to her about it and even suggested a couple of books about abusive relationships, but she would never admit she'd been hit."

"Had you ever noticed bruising or injuries before or after that incident?"

Edna shook her head. "No. Frannie never showed any sign of abuse before that black eye. And while she was skittish for a few weeks after, she seemed to recover emotionally as she did physically. If I had to guess, I'd say whoever abused her wasn't a part of her life for long."

Chapter 11

We gathered at the main house as arranged for the Mastermind meeting. We'd decided to eat first and then discuss the case, so I buttered the garlic bread while Clara made a salad. I'd made the lasagna earlier in the day, so it had already been baking in the over for almost an hour.

"Something smells fantastic," Jack said as he came in through the back door and kissed me on the cheek.

"It's the lasagna. Why did you come in through the back door?"

"I wanted to take another look at the big cabin on the beach. I know you thought I was kidding when I said I might think about selling my house and moving to the resort, but it's been on my mind quite a bit recently."

I glanced at Clara, who took a cue from the subject and quietly left us alone. "You're seriously thinking of moving into that tiny cabin?"

"Maybe. If you stay and the resort remains a writers' colony. I spoke to the building department, and they said I shouldn't have any problem getting a permit to add on a second bedroom, which I'd use as an office. The cabin already has a huge living area and a separate bedroom and bath. There's room for the loft overhead to be expanded as well. I'd have to put a lot of my stuff in storage, but it might be worth it if it meant I could be right on the beach. Besides, it's a lot closer to the newspaper."

I tried not to frown, but I couldn't quite help it. "I understand what you're saying. And cabin twenty is in an ideal location. But are you sure you want to downsize quite that much?"

Jack came over to where I was standing and wrapped his arms around my waist from behind, pulling me against his chest. "I don't want to put any pressure on you to make a decision about New York, but if you stay, the idea of coming home to you every night holds a certain appeal. I thought of asking you to move into the house with me, but I know if you stay on Gull Island you'll want to live here. There's something really perfect about the resort and the family you've created."

"Yeah, but selling your house seems like such a huge step. The cabin doesn't even have a garage. What will you do with your car? It's much too nice to leave outside."

"I can sell the car and drive the truck. Or I can keep the house and use the garage. It's not like I need the money from the sale."

I turned so I was facing Jack and put my arms around his neck. "I love the idea of you being so close by. And if you want to renovate the cabin, it's fine with me. Technically, the decision is up to Garrett— he owns the property, after all—but I can't imagine he'd care if you wanted to pay for an addition to the structure."

"So, New York…?"

I thought about Jack coming home to the resort every night. I thought about having dinner together and walking on the beach. I thought of the family of writers that had come together to share their lives and the holiday meals that were now a part of my life. I thought of the Mastermind group and the fun we had together. Did I really want to give it all up for the job of a lifetime?

Then I thought of New York. I would have a fabulous job, but I'd be going home every night to an empty apartment. I thought of solitary meals and solitary holidays. I guess I'd needed the time I'd taken, but in the end, I knew what my choice would be all along.

"I don't suppose you're hiring at the paper?"

Jack raised a brow. "Are you looking for a job?"

"I guess if I'm going to stay, I'll need one. Garrett's coming home and the renovation is almost done."

Jack kissed me hard on the lips. "I'm very definitely hiring at the paper. At least I am for the right person."

The timer on the oven beeped, interrupting the intimate embrace that, given the fact the house was full, probably should have been interrupted anyway. We enjoyed our family meal and all gathered in the living room to discuss the case.

"Okay, who wants to start?" I asked when we were all settled.

"I'll go." Brit raised her hand. "My report's short and sweet because I don't have any news. I've been too busy to do anything."

"Ditto," Alex said.

"That's okay," I said. "I know you've both been busy and I wasn't expecting you'd be able to do much with this case."

"I have something," George spoke next. "It took some doing, but I was able to track down the original articles written by Henry Post in the mid-nineteen-sixties. I compared the stories to news reports about the Strangler, and while I can't say for certain, I think there's a good chance either the Strangler wrote the stories or he told them to someone who did."

"And Frannie...?" I asked.

"Her story wasn't included. This is the first real indication we have that her murder may have been carried out by a copycat."

"Yeah, but who?" Brit asked.

"And how did they know about the pentagram?" Alex added.

"I don't know," George answered.

"If Frannie really was murdered by someone she knew, we need to figure out a way to narrow down the suspect list," Jack commented. "So far, we've spoken to several individuals who knew Frannie, but we haven't developed a list of people with motive and opportunity that we feel could have ended Frannie's life."

"I agree with Jack," I said. "We need to focus in a bit."

"Where do we start?" Vikki asked.

Good question.

"Maybe it's time to see if Rick will let us get a peek at the original report generated by the FBI at the time of Frannie's murder," I said. I looked at Vikki. "Is he back from training?"

"He came back this afternoon. I know he plans to be in the office tomorrow to catch up on the paperwork that piled up while he was away."

"Okay, I'll call him to set up a time to speak to him," I said. "As for suspects, we still have Frannie's husband, Tom, as a viable suspect, although I have no idea how we'd prove or disprove it. Jack and I found out she was intimately involved with three men. The first was married and admitted she asked him for ten thousand dollars after their fling, which he gave her; the second didn't mention a payout, but he was single, so he may not have felt the need to hide their dalliance."

"Maybe she came back to the man from fling number one looking for more money and he killed her," Brit suggested.

"This man has an alibi, but I do think exploring the blackmail angle could be worth our while. Frannie's friend Sherry said she didn't know the identity of the third man, but I'll chat with her again. Given what we've learned, I wouldn't be a bit surprised to learn there were more than three men. Maybe a lot more. We've also learned Frannie told Sherry she was pregnant shortly before she died."

"If she was pregnant, she might have been looking for a big payout," Brit suggested. "I think the mystery man who fathered her child could be a real suspect."

I got out the whiteboard we used when researching cases and started the list. I put Tom

Kettleman on the top, followed by the man who fathered her baby. Then I added a question mark, indicating that Frannie could very well have had additional lovers we didn't yet know about.

"What about the man from the photo we found?" Clara asked.

"I took a closer look at it and realized the man's features are too typical. Unless we find an angle with a face, I don't think we can know, although one of the men I mentioned earlier, who admitted to having an affair with Frannie, could very well be the man in the photo based on his features and coloring."

"Is there a particular reason you aren't naming this man?" Alex asked.

I shrugged. "Not really, other than that he asked me not to give out his name in connection with his fling with Frannie. He seems to have an ironclad alibi and I don't suspect him of Frannie's murder, so I don't see a reason to out him. If things change and we suspect he may have been involved in Frannie's murder, of course I'll name him."

"It looks like a pretty thin list," Vikki commented. "This murder may go unsolved unless we're able to find someone who knows something and is willing to talk about it."

"Yeah, I agree. Solving the case at this point is a long shot," I said. "I found out today that Frannie had facial injuries consistent with being beaten. If we can find out who beat her up and why, we might come across a motive for murder we aren't yet aware of."

"Okay, then; let's just keep asking around and see what pops," Jack suggested.

After the meeting broke up, I pulled Vikki aside to let her know I'd decided to turn down the job in

New York. I was surprised at how happy and relieved she was. I'd thought she was a bit more neutral, but maybe, like Jack, she was simply trying to give me the space I needed.

Jack and I left the house to take a walk along the beach. When we got to cabin 20, we stopped to take a look at it. It was right on the sand and fairly isolated from the other cabins, which was nice. The turtles nested each year in the dunes nearby, and it would be nice to have someone in the cabin who I could trust to respect their space. Garrett and I had chatted about how important it would be to find exactly the right person for this very important cabin, which still hadn't undergone renovations. It needed a lot of work, but Jack had plenty of money and he'd already proven he was good with a hammer too. If he put his mind to it, cabin 20 would be ready to move in to before spring and the return of the turtles.

"The more I think about it, the more I think I might raise the roofline over the loft and use it as an office. I still want to add a second bedroom; it never hurts to have a guest room. The downstairs space is large enough for a sofa and an entertainment center. I'd like to add a fireplace and maybe some additional windows. I won't be able to bring my piano with me, but I can keep the house and leave the piano there, sell it, or put it in storage." Jack grabbed my hand. "I'm really excited about this."

"And I'll be very happy to have you close by, but are you sure? It'll be quite a change."

"I'm really sure. People on the outside looking in at what I have up there on the bluff may not understand why I'd want to move into a cabin smaller than my current living room, but living alone in a big house can feel empty and lonely. I love being here at the resort and I love being with you."

I stopped walking. "Okay, so say you sell your house. Say you uproot your whole life and move out to the resort. What happens if we don't work out?"

Jack frowned. "You don't think we'll work out?"

"I do think we will. But we've only been dating for three months. I just want to be sure you've considered all the angles before you make such a big move."

Jack stared into the distance. "Fair enough. I guess if we don't work out as a couple, I hope we'll still be friends and it won't be strange for me to live here. If for some reason we can't be friends, I can move. I have a lot of money. I can buy a new house any time I want. I don't want you to worry about me having a degree of certainty. I'm comfortable with having a little uncertainty in my life."

I bowed my head. "Okay, then. If you're sure, I think your idea is a good one. It'll be nice having you in my everyday life."

"Great. Then I'll stop by to talk to Garrett tomorrow." Jack stopped and looked around. "Did you hear a noise?"

"A noise?"

"Shh," Jack said and then just listened. "It sounds like someone's crying."

I listened carefully. "I do hear something." I pointed down the beach. "That way."

Jack and I walked down the beach, listening for the sound along the way. When we'd walked about fifty yards we heard it again, only louder.

"It sounds like a dog." I walked toward the marsh. I knew animals occasionally became tangled in fishing lines.

"Over there." Jack pointed to a spot where a golden retriever puppy was trapped inside a crab trap that must have washed up onto the beach.

"Poor thing. Is she hurt?"

Jack worked the door of the trap open and gently lifted the pup out. The trap was perhaps two feet by two feet, and high enough so the puppy could sit up, but I could see she was cold and scared.

"It doesn't look like she's hurt. Let's get her back to the house and take a closer look."

Jack unzipped his jacket and stuffed the puppy inside. Then he zipped the jacket back up so only her head stuck out.

"I wonder how she ended up out here," I said. "We're a long way from any neighborhoods."

"She might have been dumped. It happens, unfortunately. If she doesn't appear to be hurt, I'll take her to the veterinarian tomorrow for a checkup. And I'll post notices that she's been found, just in case."

By the time we got back to the house the puppy had stopped shivering and it was evident there was a new girl in Jack's life I'd have to compete with for his affections. Not that I minded. The pup was adorable, and Jack looked like he'd just won the lottery. I wondered why he'd never had a dog before. Maybe he'd been waiting for the perfect moment, when everything seemed to be coming together.

Chapter 12

Wednesday, December 20

It had been five days since the Mastermind meeting. I'd called Margo on Saturday to let her know that while I was very grateful for the offer, I wouldn't be taking the job. She wasn't all that surprised after speaking to Dru, who'd shared with her his opinion that my life in New York was a thing of the past and I seemed very happy and content on Gull Island.

Jack had taken Kizmet to the vet and she was fine. At first, I wasn't sure about the name, but Jack insisted the name, which meant destiny or fate, was perfect for the puppy he was sure we were meant to share our life with. Of course, Jack just ended up calling her Kizzy most of the time, which I thought was completely adorable.

Jack had met with Garrett about the plans for the cabin. He was thrilled to have someone as responsible as Jack moving into the environmentally sensitive space, and the two had been talking blueprints ever since.

I asked Sherry about the possibility of additional men in Frannie's life. She maintained that she didn't know of anyone else with any certainty, though she suspected Frannie had been having a fling with someone who also lived at the resort. For a moment I once again suspected my father, but then I realized he'd already left the island before Frannie was murdered, and if he'd simply been sleeping with her, I really didn't want to know. In terms of a suspected killer, it looked as if our list was down to Tom or the man who'd fathered her baby. While I couldn't quite put my finger on it, I had a niggling feeling there was something important I knew but wasn't considering. Rick, or as I often refer to him, Deputy Savage, had agreed to ask the FBI for an original, complete copy of the FBI file relating to Frannie's death. After a bit of negotiating, he'd managed to obtain it, and Jack and I planned to meet with him later that afternoon to go over it.

After some additional discussion, we decided Garrett would, indeed, come to the resort on Thursday to begin his Christmas holiday. I was excited to have him home and I knew he was excited too. I just hoped everything would go well enough so he'd return to the resort permanently. I'd bought some new bedding to brighten his room and we'd moved Blackbeard's overnight cage into the room so the two buddies could be close to each other.

Clara had developed the baking bug, so I'd agreed to pick up some additional supplies while I was in town. The goodies were all wonderful, but if she didn't cut back on the pastries I found impossible to resist, I wasn't going to be able to fit into my skinny jeans much longer.

"Have you seen my black pumps?" Brit asked after jogging down the stairs from the second story of the main house.

"No. Why?"

"I can't find them and I need them for the play. I haven't worn them in months, but I've searched my cabin from top to bottom and they aren't there. I hoped I'd left them here, but they aren't in my old room."

"I'm sorry, Brit. I haven't seen them, but I'll keep an eye out for them."

"Thanks. I hate to spend any of my dwindling savings on shoes I'll most likely only wear once or twice a year."

"How's the play going?"

"I'll admit to a few opening-night jitters, but overall, it's all going well. We're sold out for the entire run, so it's a good thing you bought your tickets early. By the way, before I got distracted by the shoes, I meant to tell you I met a man at the dress rehearsal last night who's eighty-six and has lived on Gull Island his entire life. I asked him if he remembered a woman named Frannie and he said he did."

My eyes grew large. "Really? Do you think he'd speak to us?"

"He said he would. I have his number." Brit pulled a piece of paper from her pocket and handed it to me. "Just tell him that you're my friend. And if you find the shoes, text me. If I don't find them soon, I'll need to run to the store to buy another pair."

Five minutes after Brit left, it occurred to me to look in my own closet. Clara liked to tidy up and I'd noticed that on occasion, when I'd left my shoes downstairs, they'd somehow magically appeared in my closet the next time I looked. It was possible she had mistaken Brit's shoes for mine if the they'd been left lying around at some point. Sure enough, I found the shoes. I texted Brit to let her know I'd drop them by her cabin on my way into town to fetch the supplies Clara needed for the next decadent creation she had planned.

******

By the time I returned from town with Clara's things, the man Brit had told me about had returned my call. Walter Thompson had moved to the island when he was just four years old. His father had been a fisherman who used Gull Island as his port of call. Mr. Thompson insisted I call him Walt. He invited me to come by and after a brief introduction on both our parts, Walt and I settled in to chat.

"The island has changed quite a bit since I first arrived," Walt began in a deep baritone voice.

"I imagine it has."

"And not necessarily for the better. There was a time the island had more open space than developed areas, but it seems the opposite is true these days."

"I've only lived here since June and I came from New York City, so it feels pretty open to me, but I understand what you're saying. It does seem there's a lot of new construction."

"Hard to make a living fishing these days. I guess tourism has taken over. It's a shame, but I guess progress is inevitable. So, Miss Brit told me you had some questions about Frannie K."

"I do. And I appreciate you taking the time to speak to me. I guess you know Frannie was found dead in a cemetery fifty miles from here a little over a year after she moved to the island."

"I remember. They said the Strangler got her."

"Yes, that was the official finding. My friends and I are taking a second look at the case. It's our opinion that Frannie may have died at the hands of someone other than the Strangler. We don't really have a lot to go on, so we're talking to people who lived on the island at the time she died who may have known her, or at least known something about her."

"Frannie was a pretty little thing. She lived out at the Hanford place. I won't claim to have known her well, but I owned a bar back then, and she stopped by for some company now and again."

"Did she arrive alone?" I asked.

"Most of the time, although she never left alone. Frannie didn't drink and she wasn't wild like some, but she did have a taste for men. She'd come in every couple of months and scope the place out. If she found someone she liked, she'd approach him. Frannie had an infectious smile, so more often than not, she'd end up leaving with whoever she'd picked out."

"Can you remember the names of any of those men?"

"Sure. A few. Although most of the men who come to mind have died or moved away by now."

"Yes, researching such an old case has been challenging. Would you mind sharing the names of the ones you can remember?"

Walt paused. "You think one of those men might have killed her?"

"I don't know. To be honest, we don't have a lot of leads, so we're following every path we come across."

"And you're sure it wasn't the Strangler who got her?"

"Sure, no. We do have reason to suspect Frannie wasn't one of the Strangler's victims, however. The only way we'll ever know for certain is to find someone who knows what really happened the night Frannie died."

"I do know something that might help you. I tried to tell the young FBI agent who was looking into things what I'd seen, but he didn't seem much interested."

"What did you see?" I asked.

"I took a break from the bar and went out to the parking lot for a smoke the night before I heard Frannie's body had been found. Frannie was in the parking lot, talking to a tall man with blond hair. They seemed to be arguing. I headed over and asked her if she was okay and she said she was. She thanked me for checking on her and then she followed the man to his car. They were sitting there talking when I went back indoors, but neither of them came inside."

"And the FBI agent wasn't interested in what you had to say?"

"Nope. He said they already knew Frannie died as a result of being strangled by this mass murderer everyone was after. I pointed out that maybe the man I saw was him, but they said the man they were after had dark hair and a dark complexion."

I frowned. The dark hair/dark complexion point was new information, but to totally disregard the fact that a witness had seen Frannie just hours before her death seemed insane to me. "Did you tell the FBI agent anything else?"

"Just that Frannie came in often and tended to leave with different men when she did. I was the one to ask to speak to the man in charge of the investigation, not the other way around. I got the feeling right off the bat that he wasn't happy about being bothered. I know when a person is listening to what I have to say and when he isn't, so after a bit I left and got on with my life."

"I don't blame you. That must have been frustrating. It seems as if you saw the man who killed Frannie. If I showed you some photos, would you still recognize him?"

"Yup. I suppose I would."

"I'll see if I can find photos of our suspects and call you for another appointment when I have what I need."

"Okay. That'd be fine. I'd like to help if there's still a killer out there thinking he got away with killing that poor girl."

I left Walt's house and headed to the newspaper to visit with Jack and Kizmet. Jack had been taking the puppy to work with him every day and the cute little girl had quickly become the official *Gull Island News* mascot.

"Kizzy." I bent down to greet the bundle of fur who'd run over to cover me with kisses the moment I walked through the door.

"Maybe I should have gotten my kiss first." Jack laughed as he kissed me hard on the lips. "How did your interview go?"

"I think we might actually have something." I explained what Walt had seen on the night she died. "Do you think you can find a photo of Tom Kettleman on the internet?"

Jack shrugged. "I can try. He was in the military, so I might be able to find one associated with his service to his country. Perhaps there was a mention in his hometown paper when he went off to Vietnam, or even an obituary. Not all small-town newspapers have digitized their back issues, but some have."

"Great. If you can find a photo, I'll show it to Walt. If she was with Tom that night, it's likely he really did kill his wife."

Jack sat down at the computer and started to work while I sat on the carpet and played with the puppy. I'd never had a dog and didn't think I'd even wanted one, but this little girl certainly had captured my heart. She was sweet and playful but knew when to be quiet and still. I wasn't sure how old she was, but one thing was true: she was a lot mellower than most puppies.

"I've got something," Jack said after only a couple of minutes.

"That was fast." I stood up, and Kizzy waddled over to her bed to watch from the sidelines.

"I found a wedding photo of Frannie and Tom. It looks like they married a week before he shipped out, although the article says they'd known each other for years."

I looked at the photo. Neither of them were smiling, which I found odd. "Can you print it?"

Jack hit a button. "Done."

"I'll take it by to show to Walt after we speak to Savage." I glanced at Kizzy. "What do we do with her while we're out?"

"We'll only be gone for an hour. She'll be fine napping in her crate."

Deputy Savage was waiting for us with the file we were interested in on his desk when we arrived. We took a few minutes to catch him up on what we'd learned to date before asking him what he made of the notes he'd managed to obtain.

"Based on what I've read," Rick began, "it appears the officer who responded to the call realized immediately that Mrs. Kettleman was the fourth victim of the Strangler. He called the FBI, who sent an agent to check it out. The agent agreed. As far as I can tell, no other suspects were considered, and a local investigation was never initiated. It was only a week later that the Strangler's fifth victim was discovered, and the entire focus of the FBI was to find the man responsible for so many deaths."

Savage pushed the file across the desk.

I grabbed the file and opened it. I had a hunch Rick was correct about not getting much from it, but I wanted to look for myself. The entire file dealt with the identity of the Strangler and hunches the agents followed in their search for him, but there hadn't been many interviews conducted on the island.

"It says here the special agent in charge on Gull Island was Brice Jeffries," I said.

"Yes, that's correct, but if you're thinking it might be a good idea to track him down to interview him, I already did. He died four years ago."

"That isn't why I mentioned his name. It sounds familiar."

"It's doubtful anyone in town would know him. He didn't live on the island and didn't visit even at the time of Frannie's death. He sent a man named Phillip Snyder to ask around a bit, but that was pretty much the extent of the local investigation."

"That might be, but the name's familiar. Maybe Ned mentioned him. He did say he'd spoken to the investigator, even though he wasn't asked to help."

Savage nodded. "Yeah, that's probably it. I didn't think about Ned."

"I guess we'll just keep following the leads we have. I have a feeling, though, that this is one mystery we may not solve."

We left Savage's office and Jack went back to the newspaper to check on Kizzy while I drove to Walt's house for the second time that day. I brought him three photos to look at, of Tom Kettleman, Clint Brown, and Roland Carver. Clint had said he'd provided an alibi to the FBI, but the more I considered this case, the less confident I was that the FBI had checked it out.

"Nope," Walt said when I showed him the photos. "I recognize this one as Clint Brown and this as Roland Carver. Both of them did tend to have wandering eyes, and I'd heard they might have had flings with Frannie, but neither are the man I saw her with." Walt held one photo a bit closer to his face to get a better look. "The man I saw did have the same coloring and similar features to Roland, however. If you stumble across a man who looks a lot like Roland but isn't him, you might just have your man."

Chapter 13

I was pretty down by the time I headed back to the newspaper. I knew going in to this case that solving it was going to be a long shot, but I still felt somewhat deflated at hitting a total roadblock. The only person left on our list was the father of Frannie's baby, assuming she'd really been pregnant. I realized all we had as proof for that was the word of Frannie's friend Sherry, and the only proof *she* had was Frannie's say-so. Surely they'd done an autopsy, and surely the autopsy would answer that question one way or another.

Deciding I needed that information sooner rather than later, I changed direction in midtrip and headed back to Savage's office. Luckily, he was still at his desk. I asked about the autopsy and he handed me the file, saying he had work to do, but I was welcome to peruse the file to my heart's content. It took a while, but I finally found what I was looking for. Frannie had been almost three months pregnant when she died. Could the man she'd been with outside the bar been the father of her child? Might she have made demands he wasn't willing to meet? Could he have killed her?

Of course, if the man who killed Frannie was the father of her baby that didn't explain how he knew about the pentagram. Unless…

I looked once more at the name of the FBI agent. Brice Jeffries. Hadn't Roland Carver said one of the men in the photo in his home was named Brice? I remembered he was tall and thin and had light hair much like Roland's. Playing a hunch, I left the sheriff's office and set out for Roland's house again.

"You're back," Roland said when he opened the door.

"I wanted to ask if I could take another look at the photo in your den. In fact, I'd like to take a photo of it with my phone, if you don't mind."

Roland stepped aside and I entered. I followed him down the hall to the room where we'd spoken the last time.

"Do you want to tell me why you want to take a picture of the photo?"

"I found someone who saw a man with Frannie on the night she died. He didn't know him, but he feels he'd be able to recognize him if he saw a photo of him." I paused to look at the photo and frowned.

"So, you think either Kurt, Brice, Clint, or I killed Frannie? I already told you neither Brice nor Kurt lived on the island, and I had no reason to kill her."

I continued to study the photo. "I don't think it was you who killed Frannie. I thought it might be Brice." I looked at the photo more closely. "It seems someone named Brice Jeffries was the FBI agent working on the Strangler case. It occurred to me that if Brice was the killer, it would explain how the killer knew about the pentagram on the victim's shoulder. But now that I've taken a second look, I don't think so. My witness said the man wasn't you but looked a lot like you. Brice has similar coloring but a very different overall look."

I glanced at the man between Roland and Brice. Roland had said he was his brother, Kurt. He'd invited Brice, who had never sailed, to the event because they needed a fourth, and they knew each other from work. If they knew each other from work, and Brice worked for the FBI, that meant ...

"It was Kurt," I blurted out. "He looks just like you and he also worked for the FBI." I turned and looked at Roland. "Did you know?"

I could tell by the expression on his face that he had. Suddenly, I realized confronting Roland alone in his home hadn't been the smartest thing to do, even though he was a lot older than me and seemed harmless enough.

"Why didn't you tell someone what you knew?" I demanded.

A look of remorse crossed Roland's face. "I thought about telling Ned what had happened, but that wouldn't bring Frannie back, and Kurt was my brother. I loved him. And I knew Frannie was a flirt who would sleep with any man. Once she was done with them, she'd toss them aside, though not before demanding money for her services. I knew the score and paid her willingly, but Kurt fell in love with her. I mean really, deeply in love. I tried to warn him that she didn't return his affection, but he wouldn't listen. When she came to him for money to pay for an abortion, he begged her to marry him. When reminded him that she was already married, he begged her to run away with him. When she laughed in his face and told him that she'd had her fun with him and never wanted to see him again, he went a little crazy."

"I guess I could see how your brother could have acted in rage."

"He was a good man who let that witch send him over the edge. They struggled and he hit her over the head. When he realized what he'd done, he panicked and called me. By the time I arrived, Frannie was already dead. I was scared for him, so I came up with the idea to make it look like the Strangler had killed Frannie. Kurt had been working the case, so he knew all the specifics. As it turned out, we got a few things wrong, but as the special agent working the case, Kurt swept them under the rug, and in the end, everyone thought the Strangler really had killed her. I hoped that would be the end of it, but it wasn't. At least not for Kurt. He couldn't deal with the fact that he'd killed not only the woman he loved, but his own child. He fell into a deep depression, started drinking, and, eventually, lost his job. He would have ended up on the street if I hadn't helped him out. There was a part of me that felt burdened by what I'd done, and there were times I considered going to Ned, but Kurt was suffering enough. I didn't see the point of punishing him further."

"But…" I stopped myself. Now wasn't the time to argue with Roland. I'd walk away and let Savage handle it. "You know what? You're right. I didn't grow up with a sibling, but if I had, I'd probably do whatever it took to protect them. I wanted to solve this mystery, but now I realize there isn't any point. Everyone involved is dead."

I'd just begun to turn to the door when I saw Roland had a small gun in his hand. I froze.

"I can't let you go. You know too much. If you tell the authorities I knew Kurt was the killer and chose to cover it up, it will be *me* in prison. I'm an old man and that's not how I want to spend the rest of my time on earth."

I took a deep breath, trying not to panic. "I won't tell. I promise."

Roland actually paused. I could see he wanted to believe me but couldn't. "I'm sorry. I can't take that chance."

"So you're going to shoot me?"

"No, I'm not going to do that either. For now, I'm going to lock you up until I can decide what to do with you. Put your bag and your cell phone on the table."

I did as I was told.

"Now continue down the hall."

Roland led me to a basement room. It was dreary, built from cylinder blocks, without windows. There were a stack of blankets in a corner.

"Light on or off?'

"On, please."

He turned on the light, then closed the door, locking it from the outside. I took another deep breath and once again tried not to panic. I wasn't sure what Roland was going to do with me, but I was in no immediate danger. I looked around the room, but it was obvious there was no way out. I suspected it was soundproof, so screaming wasn't going to do me any good. All I could do was wait for Roland to return or hope someone would rescue me though no one other than he knew I was here.

Despite the lack of windows, the room seemed to have fresh air. It was a bit on the chilly side, but I could curl up with the blankets, and I found a few cans of food on a shelf. All in all, it wasn't a horrible place to be trapped for a few hours. If Roland decided just to leave me here, however, would anyone ever find me?

No, I decided, just waiting wasn't an option. The problem was, I didn't have a better plan. I wished Roland hadn't thought to take my phone. I was fairly certain I wasn't going to find a means of communication among the supplies stacked on the shelves, but looking gave me something to do.

The longer I searched with zero results, the angrier I got. Just when things were coming together, it would be so unfair if I wasn't alive to enjoy it. Jack and I were in such a good place, and I was excited about working with him at the newspaper. Kizzy was adorable and I was starting to love her already. It was almost like having a child with Jack. Garrett was doing better and would be coming home, and I had a feeling he and Clara might be destined for each other. Vikki and Rick seemed to have found a common ground and George was happy with Meg. It was almost Christmas and love was in the air. I wanted to be there to enjoy it.

"Damn," I said aloud as I hit the wall with my hand. When I saw blood on my knuckles, I realized how stupid that had been. I grabbed a blanket, walked across the room, and sat on the floor near the door. Waiting appeared to be all I could do after all.

To occupy my mind with something other than my dire predicament, I turned my mind to Secret Santa. I'd decided not to try to publish an article outing the guy, but I was still curious. Evan Paddington was still my number-one suspect, but I'd learned over the past week that he was in Europe, which was why he hadn't returned my call, and it seemed to me Secret Santa would stay closer to home with the big day just around the corner. I supposed Evan could have someone helping him. Being out of town when the annual Christmas miracle occurred would take the focus off him if he didn't want to be found out and worried there were people like me who suspected him. Still, the gifts were always well thought out and personal. You'd think he'd want to be here to see the expression on the face of the recipient.

And then there was the sheer amount of money spent. I did a quick tally, and over the past twelve years, Secret Santa must have spent close to a half million dollars. Some years the gift would have required a lesser amount—maybe ten or twenty thousand dollars—but others were much more significant, with Secret Santa paying off debts or donating real estate. Evan had inherited money, but I had no idea how much.

"There has to be a way out of here," I mumbled to myself as I gave up thinking about Evan and began to pace again. Maybe I could work the lock on the door loose if I pounded on it, or if I screamed loud enough, someone would hear me.

The longer I paced, the more panicked I began to feel. I wasn't sure how much time had passed, but I figured Jack would be looking for me by now. He would most likely have alerted Savage, and at some point, the deputy would think to look at the report I'd been studying. If I could link the name of the FBI agent in charge of the Strangler investigation to the man in Roland's photo, with enough time, Jack would as well.

I wondered if Roland had left the house or he was still upstairs. Had he thought to move my car or turn off my cell? If he hadn't turned off the phone, Savage could ping it. Both Jack and Rick Savage were intelligent men. They'd figure it out eventually.

It wasn't a lot later before I heard movement upstairs. I hesitated for a moment, not knowing who was responsible for the sounds, but I decided I'd waited long enough and began to scream. Several seconds later, Rick and Jack crashed through the door.

Jack wrapped me in his arms and I fought off tears of relief. "Roland's brother killed Frannie," I blurted out.

"He isn't here," Rick informed me.

"The marina. Try the marina. There's no way he'd leave the island for good without his boat."

Chapter 14

Friday, December 22

Brit's *A Christmas Carol* was better than anything I could have imagined. It was sweet and funny and really brought home the feeling of Christmas. Brit played Mrs. Cratchit, and she only had a few lines, but her facial expressions as she stood in the background while her husband, Bob, was speaking to Mr. Scrooge, were priceless.

It had been a crazy couple of days, but things were settling down at last, and I was ready to get on with the festivities. The main house was decorated, gifts had been purchased and wrapped, the baking complete, and food for the weekend bought and stored.

Rick had caught up with Roland at the marina, as I suggested. He'd confessed to his part in the cover-up of Frannie's murder and was spending the holiday in jail. I wasn't sure how things would work out, but I hoped he'd be able to cut a deal with the district attorney to avoid time in prison, as he'd feared. He was an old man and all he'd done was to protect his brother. He may not have made the right choice, but a lot of people would have done the same thing in his place.

Garrett was home and settled in his room, and he and Blackbeard seemed over-the-top happy to be together again. Garrett was able to get around fine on his own between his walker and his wheelchair. I wanted this visit to go well so Garrett would be confident enough make arrangements to move back to the resort for good.

Clara was delighted to have Garrett in the house. They'd spent a lot of time playing cards and watching old Christmas movies. When she wasn't with Garrett, Clara spent most of her time baking, which was working out fine because Garrett loved sweets.

Brit and George were packed and ready to fly out to spend the weekend with their family. They hadn't visited in quite some time, so I was glad they'd planned this trip for the long holiday. Rick had come to the house for the dinner we were preparing and Vikki still intended to go home with him for the weekend, and Alex was packed for his trip to the Bahamas.

And Jack had settled into my room at the resort, planning to stay for several days at least. We'd brought Kizzy's crate and set it up in my room, so I felt like my little family was set for the holiday.

I'd received a text from Dru, letting me know he'd had a good time on Gull Island and hoped we'd stay in touch. I'd assured him I'd like that too, and then I sent a text to Margo wishing her a happy holiday. I hoped she wasn't too angry with me for turning down her offer. She'd sounded as if she understood when I'd spoken to her, but she'd gone out of her way to give me a second chance at my career and I wanted to be sure she knew how much I appreciated it. Maybe I'd make a trip to New York after the first of the year to ensure those important people knew how much they meant to me.

I was excited and hopeful about what the future might bring. In fact, I couldn't remember a time when I was quite as content as I was at that very minute.

******

We congratulated Brit on a job well done and returned to the resort, where Vikki helped Clara and George get dinner on the table, while Jack and I each grabbed a flashlight and took our new baby Kizzy for a walk. I loved to watch her run and play, and she was such a good puppy, she came when you called her and rarely barked. Sadly, Agatha and Blackbeard both hated her quite a lot, though their mutual hatred of the puppy seemed to have helped them to forge a bond and had all but stopped picking on each other.

Jack spent the first part of the walk talking about the cabin he wanted to remodel. He was now thinking of tearing down the cabin closest to 20 so he'd have absolute privacy, and he'd upgraded the remodel to a four-bedroom unit with an expanded loft. What he wanted all that room for I didn't know, and when I asked him about it he didn't answer, but I noticed a gleam in his eye that made my heart beat just a tiny bit faster.

Of course, Jack would pay Garrett handsomely for the use of the land, and now my brother was talking about adding a pool to the property. At first, I didn't know why he would need a pool when the ocean was so close, but he'd pointed out that it would be good for his physical therapy, which made a lot of sense.

"It sure is a beautiful night," Jack said as we paused to look at the reflection of the moon on the sea.

"It is. I'm glad we decided to take a few minutes to ourselves. It's been a very hectic week."

"It has, but I only have one more thing to take care of and then I'm yours for the whole weekend."

"One more thing?" I asked.

Jack winked. "It's a secret."

I looked directly at Jack. "Are you Secret Santa?"

Jack feigned shock. "Whyever would you think that?"

"It just occurred to me that the amount of money that's been spent on the Secret Santa projects over the past twelve years has been substantial. There aren't a lot of people on the island who would have the bank to do all that."

"I guess that's a good point."

"So, *are* you Secret Santa?"

"Are you still intent on unmasking the holiday crusader?"

"No. There's something very special about the secret part of the acts that have been carried out. I'm just curious."

Jack took my hand and started to walk again. "All right. The answer to your question is a story, if you'll bear with me."

"Fine."

"When I was just starting out with my writing, I let the fame part of what I was doing go to my head. I'd written a couple of *New York Times* best sellers and I was riding the fame train, which led to guest spots on all the big talk shows, invites to parties and premieres, more money than I could reasonably manage, and, of course, women. Lots and lots of women."

"Go on, but skip the part about the women. I don't need to know the specifics."

"What it really comes down to is, by the time I was working on my fifth book, I had a very full social life. I also had my fair share of stalkers and paparazzi to deal with."

"Stalkers?"

"Not the dangerous sort. I'm talking about fans who'd wait outside my apartment building to catch me coming and going, and the line of autograph seekers that formed when I tried to dine out. The result was that I was having a hard time meeting my contractual deadline. My editor knew I was struggling, so he suggested I take a break from the media circus. He got me together with Valerie McCall, who had a cabin on Gull Island. She offered me the use of it while I finished my manuscript and I accepted."

"I spoke to her. She seems really nice."

"She is very nice. She invited me to use the cabin whenever I wanted, so I started spending a month here every year while I worked on my next book. During my time on the island, I tended to stay in, so I hadn't met the locals yet, but I'd fallen in love with the area."

"What does all this have to do with Secret Santa?" I asked.

"I'm getting to it. Twelve years ago, just before Christmas, a lightning strike started a fire. Four cabins burned to the ground, including Valerie's. Two of the four cabins were vacation rentals owned by investors, but the fourth cabin was owned and lived in by a family of six. After the fire, they had nowhere to go, so Valerie and I decided to anonymously rent the family a home, decorate it, and provide wrapped gifts for all the children. Trust me: at that point neither of us had any intention of becoming Secret Santa."

Jack paused and I waited. I realized where this was going, but I figured I'd let him tell the story at his own pace.

"The following year I got a call from Valerie, who'd rebuilt her cabin and was staying on the island for the holiday. She told me the local animal shelter had lost their lease and was going to have to close its doors. She'd found a warehouse she wanted to convert for use as a shelter and wondered if I wanted to team up with her again. I'd found that helping the family the year before had been wildly satisfying, so I agreed. To make a long story short, that started the tradition of the two of us teaming up to provide for someone in need during the holidays."

I reached up and kissed Jack on the lips. "I think what the two of you are doing is wonderful."

"Thanks. It's satisfying to be able to give back to the community." Jack took out his phone and glanced at it. "In fact, I need to follow up on something for this year's miracle, so let's head back."

"You go ahead. I think Kizzy and I will walk to the end of the beach."

After Jack left I took a moment to contemplate what I'd just learned. I wasn't surprised to hear Jack was Secret Santa, but I was surprised to discover how very little I really knew about him. I didn't know where our relationship would take us, but I did intend to take the time to find out a whole lot more about this man who had showed up in my life and swept me off my feet.

The Secret Santa story would have been huge if I'd been able to reveal that behind the gifts were two very popular authors. And it was too bad the whole world wouldn't know the wonderful things Jack and Valerie were doing. But the point Colin Walton had made about the reward of giving being all that much sweeter when accomplished anonymously, actually made a lot of sense.

Kizzy and I had come to the end of the beach and turned back toward the house when I noticed the light on in Nicole Carrington's cabin. I was certain I'd be snubbed for my effort, but it was Christmas and we were all having dinner, and it seemed like the right thing to do to invite her to join us, even if I was certain she'd say no. Kizzy and I climbed her front steps and knocked on the door. Nicole looked surprised to see us when she answered.

"Can I help you?" she asked.

"I know you've explained your preference not to join in group activities, but we're making dinner tonight and I thought you might like to join us. It's casual," I assured her. "Clara made a ham, George is making his famous beans, Brit is doing something with potatoes, cheese, and sour cream that smells heavenly, and Alex mixed up a pitcher of margaritas."

I waited for the negative response and was fully prepared to smile and leave, no matter how rude she was.

"Is that your dog?"

I looked down at the puppy sitting politely at my feet. "Sort of. Jack and I found her on the beach last week. She lives with Jack for the time being, but we sort of share her."

A look of longing came over Nicole's face. "I've always wanted a dog, but I've never lived anywhere that would allow me to have one."

"You're welcome to have a polite, well-trained dog, or a dog that's crated until trained while you're away from the cabin if you'd like. When Jack moves to the resort, Kizzy will be living here."

Nicole smiled. I had to admit I was so surprised, I almost commented but caught myself just in time.

"I might think about it. And yes, a well-trained dog will be a must. I wouldn't want to worry about the furniture getting chewed up."

"You might consider a rescue dog. Puppies can be a lot of work and do tend to chew, but I'm sure if you explained your needs to the local rescue workers, they could help you find the perfect companion."

Nicole looked at Kizzy again. "Thank you for the suggestion. I may have a talk with them."

"Great. I'm anxious to see who you welcome into your life." I glanced at the house. "So, about dinner…"

Nicole looked as if she was going to flee, but then Kizzy walked over and put a paw on her leg. Nicole bent down and petted the pup, who was calm and not at all rambunctious. She looked at me with an expression of uncertainty. "Okay. I guess I'm hungry, and I do like ham and beans."

It was official; Jack might be Secret Santa, a mysterious presence who brought miracles to the island, but as far as I was concerned, Kizzy convincing Nicole to take the first step toward becoming one of the group was the real Christmas miracle at the Turtle Cove Resort this year.

A New Series from Kathi Daley Books

http://amzn.to/2wHBETt

Preview Chapter 1

There are people in the world who insist that life is what you make of it. They'll tell you that if you work hard enough and persevere long enough, everything you've ever desired will one day be yours. But as I sat in the fifth dingy office I'd visited in as many months and listened as the fifth pencil pusher in a dark suit and sensible shoes looked at me with apologetic eyes, I finally understood that not every dream was realized and not every wish granted.

"Ms. Carson, do you understand what I'm saying?"

I nodded, trying to fight back the tears I absolutely would not shed. "You're saying that you can't consider my grant application unless I've secured a facility."

The man let out a long breath that sounded like a wheeze, which I was sure was more of a sigh of relief. "Exactly. I do love your proposal to build an animal shelter in your hometown, but our grant is designed to be used for ongoing operations. I'm afraid without a physical presence we really must move on."

I leaned over to pick up my eight-year-old backpack. "Yes. I understand. Thank you so much for your time."

"Perhaps next year?" the man encouraged with a lopsided grin.

I smiled in return. Granted, it was a weak little smile that did nothing to conceal my feelings of defeat. "Thank you. I'm certain we'll be able to meet your criteria by the next application cycle."

"We begin a new cycle on June 1. If you can secure a facility by that time please feel free to reapply," the man said.

I thanked the bureaucrat and left his office. I tried to ignore the feeling of dread in the pit of my stomach and instead focused on the clickety-clack that sounded as the tile floor came into contact with the two-inch heels I'd bought for this occasion. Had I really been working on this project for more than two years? Maybe it was time to throw in the towel and accept defeat. The idea of building an animal shelter in Rescue Alaska was a noble one, but the mountain of fund-raising and paperwork that needed to be scaled to make this particular dream come true seemed insurmountable at best.

I dug into my backpack for my cell phone, which rang just as I stepped out of the warm building into the bracing cold of the frigid Alaskan winter. I pulled the hood of my heavy parka over my dark hair before wrapping its bulk tightly around my small frame.

"So, how did it go?" My best friend, Chloe Rivers, asked the minute I answered her call.

"It went."

"What happened?" Chloe groaned.

I looked up toward the sky, allowing the snow to land on my face and mask my tears. "The grant is designated for operations, so it seems we aren't eligible until we have a facility. The problem is, we have no money to build a facility and no one will give us a loan for one unless we have capital for operations already lined up. It's an endless cycle I'm afraid we can't conquer."

"We can't give up. You know what you have to do."

"No," I said firmly. "We'll find another way." I knew I sounded harsh, but I had to make Chloe understand.

"Another way?" Chloe screeched. I listened as she took a deep breath before continuing in a softer tone. "Come on, Harmony, you know we've tried everything. There *is* no other way."

Chloe's plea faded as an image flashed into my mind. I closed my eyes and focused on the image before I spoke. I knew from previous experience that it was important to get a lock on the psychic connection before I said or did anything to break the spell. Once I felt I was ready, I opened my eyes and tuned back into Chloe's chatter. I was certain she hadn't missed a beat even though I'd missed the whole thing. "Look, I have to go," I interrupted. "Someone's in trouble. I'll call you later."

I hung up with Chloe, called a cab, and then called Dani Mathews. Dani was a helicopter pilot and one of the members of the search-and-rescue team I was a part of. She'd offered to give me a lift into Anchorage for my meeting today and I'd taken her up on it.

"Someone's in trouble," I said as soon as Dani answered.

"I was about to call you. I just got off the phone with Jake." Jake Cartwright was my boss, brother-in-law, and the leader of the search-and-rescue team. "There are two boys, one fifteen and the other sixteen. They'd been cross-country skiing at the foot of Cougar Mountain. Jake said they have a GPS lock on a phone belonging to one of the teens, so he isn't anticipating a problem with the rescue."

The cab pulled up and I slipped inside. I instructed the driver to head to the airport, then answered Dani. "The boys dropped the phone, so Jake and the others are heading in the wrong direction"

I slipped off my shoes as the cab sped away.

"Do you know where they are?" Dani asked with a sound of panic in her voice.

"In a cave." I closed my eyes and tried to focus on the image in my head. "The cave's shallow, but they're protected from the storm." I took off my heavy parka and pulled a pair of jeans out of my backpack. I cradled the phone to my ear with my shoulder as I slipped the jeans onto my bare legs.

"Where's the cave, Harm?"

I closed my eyes once again and let the image come to me. "I'd say they're about a quarter of a mile up the mountain."

"Are they okay?" Dani asked.

I took a deep breath and focused my energy. There were times I wanted to run from the images and feelings that threatened to overwhelm and destroy me, but I knew embracing the pain and fear was my destiny as well as my burden. "They're both scared, but only one of them is hurt. Call Jake and tell him to check the cave where we found Sitka," I said, referring to our search-and-rescue dog, who Jake and I had found lost on the mountain when he was just a puppy. "And send someone for Moose." I glanced out the window. The snow was getting heavier, and it wouldn't be long before we would be forbidden from taking off. "I'm almost at the airport. Go ahead and warm up the bird. I should be there in two minutes."

I hung up the phone and placed it on the seat next to me. The driver swerved as I pulled my dress over my head and tossed it to one side. I knew the pervert was watching, but I didn't have time to care as I pulled a thermal shirt out of my backpack, over my head, and across my bare chest.

"What's the ETA to the airport?" I demanded from the backseat.

"Less than a minute."

"Go on around to the entrance for private planes. I have the code to get in the gate. My friend is waiting with a helicopter."

As the cab neared the entrance, I pulled on heavy wool socks and tennis shoes. I wished I had my snow boots with me, but the tennis shoes would have to do because the boots were too heavy to carry around all day.

As soon as the cab stopped, I grabbed my phone, tossed some cash onto the front seat, and hopped out, leaving my dress and new heels behind.

"You've forgotten your dress, miss."

"Keep it," I said as I flung my backpack over my shoulder and took off at a full run for the helicopter. As soon as I got in, Dani took off. "Did you get hold of Jake?" I asked as I strapped myself in.

"I spoke to Sarge. He's manning the radio. He promised to keep trying to get through to Jake. The storm is intensifying at a steady rate. We need to find them."

"Moose?"

"Sarge sent someone for him."

I looked out the window as we flew toward Rescue. A feeling of dread settled in the pit of my stomach. The storm was getting stronger and I knew that when a storm blew in without much notice it caught everyone off guard, and the likelihood of a successful rescue decreased dramatically.

The team I belonged to was one of the best anywhere, our survival record unmatched. Still, I'd learned at an early age that when you're battling Mother Nature, even the best teams occasionally came out on the losing end. I picked up the team radio Dani had tucked into the console of her helicopter, pressed the handle, and hoped it would connect me to someone at the command post.

"Go for Sarge," answered the retired army officer who now worked for Neverland, the bar Jake owned.

"Sarge, it's Harmony. Dani and I are on our way, but we won't get there in time to make a difference. I need you to get a message to Jake."

"The reception is sketchy, but don't you worry your pretty head; Sarge will find a way."

"The boys are beginning to panic. I can feel their absolute horror as the storm strengthens. The one who isn't injured is seriously thinking of leaving his friend and going for help. If he does neither of them will make it. Jake needs to get there and he needs to get there fast."

"Don't worry. I'll find a way to let Jake know. Can you communicate with the boys?"

I paused and closed my eyes. I tried to connect but wasn't getting through. "I'm trying, but so far I just have a one-way line. Is Jordan there?" Jordan Fairchild was not only a member of the team but she was also a doctor who worked for the local hospital.

"She was on duty at the hospital, but she's on her way."

"Tell her she'll need to treat hypothermia." I paused and closed my eyes once again. My instinct was to block the pain and horror I knew I needed to channel. "And anemia. The break to the femur of the injured teen is severe. He's been bleeding for a while." I used the back of my hand to wipe away the steady stream of tears that were streaking down my face. God, it hurt. The pain. The fear. "I'm honestly not sure he'll make it. I can feel his strength fading, but we have to try."

"Okay, Harm, I'll tell her."

"Is Moose there?"

"He will be by the time you get here."

I put down the radio and tried to slow my pounding heart. I wasn't sure why I'd been cursed with the ability to connect psychically with those who were injured or dying. It isn't that I could feel the pain of everyone who was suffering; it seemed only to be those we were meant to help who found their way into my radar. I wasn't entirely sure where the ability came from, but I knew when I'd acquired it.

I grew up in a warm and caring family, with two parents and a sister who loved me. When I was thirteen my parents died in an auto accident a week before Christmas. My sister Val, who had just turned nineteen, had dropped out of college, returned to Rescue Alaska, and taken over as my legal guardian. I remember feeling scared and so very alone. I retreated into my mind, cutting ties to most people except for Val, who became my only anchor to the world. When I was fifteen Val married local bar owner Jake Cartwright. Jake loved Val and treated me like a sister, and after a period of adjustment, we became a family and I began to emerge from my shell. When I was seventeen Val went out on a rescue. She got lost in a storm, and although the team had tried to find her, they'd come up with nothing but dead ends. I remember sitting at the command post praying harder than I ever had before. I wanted so much to have the chance to tell Val how much I loved her. She'd sacrificed so much for me and I wasn't sure she knew how much it meant to me.

Things hadn't looked good, even though the entire team had searched around the clock. I could hear them whispering that the odds of finding her alive were decreasing with each hour. I remember wanting to give my life for hers, and suddenly, there she was, in my head. I could feel her pain, but I also knew the prayer in her heart. I knew she was dying, but I could feel her love for me and I could feel her fighting to live. I could also feel the life draining from her body with each minute that passed.

I tried to tell the others that I knew where she was, but they thought they were only the ramblings of an emotionally distraught teenager dealing with the fallout of shock and despair. When the team eventually found Val's body exactly where and how I'd told them they would, they began to believe that I really had made a connection with the only family I'd had left in the world.

Of course, the experience of knowing your sister was dying, of feeling her physical and emotional pain as well has her fear as she passed into the next life, was more than a seventeen-year-old could really process. I'm afraid I went just a bit off the deep end. Jake, who had taken over as my guardian, had tried to help me, as did everyone else in my life at the time, but there was no comfort in the world that would undo the horror I'd experienced.

And then I met Moose. Moose is a large Maine Coon who wandered into the bar Jake owned and I worked and lived in at the time. The minute I picked up the cantankerous cat and held him to my heart, the trauma I'd been experiencing somehow melted away. I won't go so far as to say that Moose has magical powers—at least not any more than I do—but channeling people in life-and-death situations is more draining than I can tolerate, and the only one who can keep me grounded is a fuzzy Coon with a cranky disposition.

"Are you okay?" Dani asked as she glanced at me out of the corner of her eye. Her concern for my mental health was evident on her face.

"I'm okay. I'm trying to connect with the boys, but they're too terrified to let me in. It's so hard to feel their pain when you can't offer comfort."

"Can't you shut if off? I can't imagine allowing myself to actually feel and experience what those boys are."

"If I block it I'll lose them. I have to hang on. Maybe I can get through to one of them. They don't have long."

"Do you really think you have the ability to do that? To establish a two-way communication?"

I put my hand over my heart. It felt like it was breaking. "I think so. I hope so. The elderly man who was buried in the avalanche last spring told me that he knew he was in his final moments and all he could feel was terror. Then I connected and he felt at peace. It was that peace that allowed him to slow his breathing. Jordan said the only reason he was still alive when we found him was because he'd managed to conserve his oxygen."

"That's amazing."

I shrugged. I supposed I did feel good about that rescue, but I'd been involved in rescues, such as Val's, in which the victim I connected with didn't make it. I don't know why it's my lot to experience death over and over again, but it seems to be my calling, so I try to embrace it so I'm available for the victims I can save like that old man.

"The injured one is almost gone," I whispered. "They need to get to him now."

I knew tears were streaming down my face as I gripped the seat next to me. The pain was excruciating, but needed to hang on.

Dani reached over and grabbed my hand. "We're almost there. I'm preparing to land. Sarge is waiting with Moose."

She guided the helicopter to the ground despite the storm raging around us. As soon as she landed, I opened the door, hopped out, and ran to the car, where Sarge was waiting with Moose. I pulled him into my arms and wept into his thick fur. Several minutes later I felt a sense of calm wash over me. I couldn't know for certain, but I felt as if the boy I was channeling had experienced that same calm. I looked at Sarge. "He's gone."

"I'm so sorry, Harm."

"The other one is still alive. He's on the verge of panicking and running out into the storm. Jake and the others have to get to him."

Sarge helped me into the car and we headed toward Neverland, where I knew the fate of the second boy would be revealed before the night came to an end.

USA Today best-selling author Kathi Daley lives with her husband, kids, grandkids, and Bernese mountain dogs in beautiful Lake Tahoe. When she isn't writing, she likes to read (preferably at the beach or by the fire), cook (preferably something with chocolate or cheese), and garden (planting and planning, not weeding). She also enjoys spending time on the water when she's not hiking, biking, or snowshoeing the miles of desolate trails surrounding her home.

Kathi uses the mountain setting in which she lives, along with the animals (wild and domestic) that share her home, as inspiration for her cozy mysteries.

Kathi is a top 100 mystery writer for Amazon and won the 2014 award for both Best Cozy Mystery Author and Best Cozy Mystery Series.

She currently writes six series: Zoe Donovan Cozy Mysteries, Whales and Tails Island Mysteries, Sand and Sea Hawaiian Mysteries, Writers' Retreat Southern Mysteries, Tj Jensen Paradise Lake Mysteries, and Seacliff High Teen Mysteries.

Giveaway:

I do a giveaway for books, swag, and gift cards every week in my newsletter, *The Daley Weekly* **http://eepurl.com/NRPDf**

Other links to check out:

Kathi Daley Blog – publishes each Friday **http://kathidaleyblog.com**

Webpage – **www.kathidaley.com**

Facebook at Kathi Daley Books – **www.facebook.com/kathidaleybooks**

Kathi Daley Books Group Page – **https://www.facebook.com/groups/569578823146850/**

E-mail – **kathidaley@kathidaley.com**

Goodreads – **https://www.goodreads.com/author/show/7278377.Kathi_Daley**

Twitter at Kathi Daley@kathidaley – **https://twitter.com/kathidaley**

Amazon Author Page –
https://www.amazon.com/author/kathidaley
BookBub – **https://www.bookbub.com/authors/kathi-daley**
Pinterest – **http://www.pinterest.com/kathidaley/**

Made in the USA
San Bernardino, CA
22 October 2017